A loaded gun.

The teargas hit me, barbed wire across my eyes, and I went down to my hands and knees, ducking all the way under it. Feet trampled each other, and one huge foot ground my hand into the asphalt as I rolled, digging my way through the mob, yelling for Bea.

That was when I touched the cold steel, wrapping my fingers around it.

I hunched over my find, kneeling on the pavement. I crouched there, waiting for the avalanche of bodies to pass, people falling over me, the breath slugged from my body.

I slipped it into my pocket.

"A psychologically intense tale of inner struggle in the face of tragedy."
—*The Bulletin of the Center for Children's Books*

"A thought-provoking story full of rich, well-developed characters." —*School Library Journal*

ALSO BY MICHAEL CADNUM

Calling Home
Breaking the Fall
Taking It
Zero at the Bone

EDGE

MICHAEL CADNUM

PUFFIN BOOKS

PUFFIN BOOKS
Published by the Penguin Group
Penguin Putnam Books for Young Readers,
345 Hudson Street, New York, New York 10014, U.S.A.
Penguin Books Ltd, 27 Wrights Lane, London W8 5TZ, England
Penguin Books Australia Ltd, Ringwood, Victoria, Australia
Penguin Books Canada Ltd, 10 Alcorn Avenue, Toronto, Ontario, Canada M4V 3B2
Penguin Books (N.Z.) Ltd, 182-190 Wairau Road, Auckland 10, New Zealand

Penguin Books Ltd, Registered Offices: Harmondsworth, Middlesex, England

First published in the United States of America by Viking,
a division of Penguin Books USA Inc., 1997
Published by Puffin Books,
a member of Penguin Putnam Books for Young Readers, 1999

1 3 5 7 9 10 8 6 4 2

THE LIBRARY OF CONGRESS HAS CATALOGED THE VIKING EDITION AS FOLLOWS:
Cadnum, Michael.
Edge: a novel / Michael Cadnum.
p. cm.
Summary: Zachary, living with his divorced mother in California,
finds violence gradually invading his life and making
significant changes in his day-to-day existence.
ISBN 0-670-87335-7 (hc.)
[1. Violence—Fiction. 2. Crime—Fiction. 3. California—Fiction.] I. Title
PZ7.C11724Ed 1997 [Fic]—dc21 96-44561 CIP AC

Puffin Books ISBN 0-14-038714-5

PRINTED IN CANADA

ONE

A bottle spun out of a car, a bright, beautiful burst against the pavement. It was dark, none of us had faces, and none of them either, headlights off, voices challenging us to come out into the street.

Earl was the one who changed everything, hopping out on one foot like a man with a peg leg, but it was only because he was getting ready to give a kick, his right leg cocked. He was dancing out there to kick a car, making a joke of it.

Everyone laughed. Even some of the refinery kids hooted, hanging out for once so we could see, faces like ours but strangers, people we would never know. But most of us didn't even know each other, kids from all over Oakland, a mix of races and attitudes. I hated all this, typical high school summer, none of us with anything better to do. I thought I had left this sort of thing behind.

When Earl went down it was because he was clumsy, kicking the rear end of a Chevy pickup and missing. He sat there afterward, looking around the way you do when you are hurt more than you expect. Or maybe he was milking the laughs.

"They hit him!"

What a thing to shout, a ragged lie, a big red headline in everybody's mind. It was me. I said it. I was sick of everyone standing around.

"Earl is hurt!" I cried. Earl did look badly hurt, once you looked at him that way, dumb with pain, his mouth slack, his head trying to look back, legs squished into place.

Look at him, I wanted to cry out.

Look at him, he's dying.

I glanced around at my feet for something to throw and lunged at the curb for a chunk of broken concrete. It was not as broken as it looked, stuck into the curb.

I dug my heel into the concrete, and it broke. I took a few running steps, brushing past people just standing there, unsure what to do. I threw the chunk as hard as I could. It punched into a car door, fragmenting.

For a moment it was all over. The concrete had burst, the car was dented. That was all. Nothing else was necessary, and we could all go home.

Then bodies poured from cars. Some of the drivers wrestled steering wheels around, deciding maybe it was time to head east along Lakeshore and take the freeway back north to the Chevron towns they came from, already having seen enough excitement.

Driving a car—especially if it's your own car, even a hulk with the chassis rusted through—sometimes makes a person feel like playing it safe.

But half the passengers were already at us, fists swinging and hitting nothing, teeth gleaming. The police were swamped, helmeted heads in a tide of grabbing, punching bodies. A helicopter pounded the air overhead, licked us all with a searchlight, and then lurched upward, gaining altitude. Sirens sang, jagged high-low notes. It was one of the reasons I had quit school, tired of the violence.

The city of Oakland chains the trash cans around Lake Merritt. You pick them up and shake them and trash tumbles out, but you can't roll the cans away or hurl them out into the street; a heavy length of chain anchors them to a tree or a light pole. Freelance recycling collectors had been there ahead of us, and only garbage was left, but I found an empty orange juice bottle, a smiling fruit wearing sunglasses on the label.

I elbowed out into the crowd with a sour, dry taste in my mouth, because things were about to get really bad, people breathing hard, faces shining with blood. It took only a few moments before people were tired and scared, not fighting now so much as shoving, and the real trouble was about to start. I didn't know what I had in mind. Maybe I was going to break the bottle and use the broken edge on someone.

At the same time, I knew this was the kind of thing I hated,

3

caught up with a bunch of kids I didn't respect, just as crazy as they were.

"I think I'm going to meet you up by the Mini Mart," Bea was saying, as loud as she could. I had to read her lips, Bea's voice lost in all the yelling and swearing, more cop cars approaching the edge of the crowd, amplified electronic commands.

She had a knit cap tugged down over her ears. "Wouldn't you like some ice cream?" she was saying: you come, too. It was just like her to state things indirectly. Bea has one of those crinkly voices. It sounds like she has to clear her throat half the time, but it's just her natural way of speaking.

I read the look in her eyes. I put down the glass bottle very carefully, knowing that someone else would knock it over or seize it and hurl it into someone's face. The cop cars have loud-speakers mounted inside, under the hoods. Cops can speak into a hand mike and the entire car is a loudspeaker announcing, *This is an illegal assembly.*

The explosion was soft, sickening, a giant water balloon. The gas was hard to see in the darkness, but the way people pan-icked surprised me, because I had seen movies where bad guys tie hankies over their faces and keep gunning down cops.

The teargas hit me, barbed wire across my eyes, and I went down to my hands and knees, ducking all the way under it. Feet trampled each other, and one huge foot ground my hand into the asphalt as I rolled, digging my way through the mob, yelling for Bea.

That was when I touched the cold steel, wrapping my fingers around it.

I hunched over my find, kneeling on the pavement. I crouched there, waiting for the avalanche of bodies to pass, people falling over me, the breath slugged from my body.

I slipped it into my pocket.

TWO

Lake Merritt is fresh water, mixed with salt tide from San Francisco Bay. The water has a smell, a room too full of people, or eggs going slightly bad. I took a moment to crouch beside the water as a family of ducks griped, looking over their feathered shoulders.

Traffic was backed up, the Oil Towners gone now, grass trampled and litter squashed out into the streets from the trash cans. My orange juice bottle was still there, a minor wonder, upright in the street.

The cops had their gas masks off, little lines on their cheeks from the pressure and the sweat. Talking into radios, writing reports. Flares had been lit on the pavement, dazzling magenta flames leaving ash like bone, and a traffic cop stood in the middle of the street, hands on his hips, watching the traffic.

I found a pay phone beside the library and got Bea's mother on the machine, her fake country western twang, "None of us are right here right now, I am very sorry to say," said Bea's mom, taking her time explaining what we could do after we heard the beep.

I hung up without leaving a message. I told myself Bea was too smart to get arrested or trampled to death.

There was no one home at Bea's house, just a front porch with bikes chained together and the TV set on a timer, CNN playing to an empty room.

A car door slammed, and there was Bea's mom in a full skirt and western boots, clumping up the slope of dried-up crabgrass. For a moment she didn't know who I was, maybe trouble waiting for her there on the porch.

"Look at you, Zachary, forlorn and lonely," she said before I could break my silence. One thing about Bea's mom, she always sounded happy. It cheered me up, sometimes, to watch her lip-sticky mouth. "Don't tell me you and Bea had a parting of the ways." Bea's mom had insisted I call her Rhonda, but I called her Mrs. Newport or else refrained from using any name at all.

"I just sort of lost track of her," I said, working on sounding casual.

"You look a little funny, Zachary," she said.

I made a casual gesture: funny, not-funny, what did it matter?

"Is Bea all right?" This was asked in a normal voice, for a second no country vanilla in her voice.

"Of course," I said. I made it sound macho: of course she's okay; she was with me.

Mrs. Newport had a solemn, stubby-looking man in tow in the darkness. She took square dancing lessons and went to Neon Leon's, a country western bar on San Pablo Avenue. She had been born and raised in South San Francisco but worked hard at her role. Her skirt looked like it had been made out of two or three red checkered tablecloths, but her blouse was pretty, little metal beads in the shape of a bucking bronco, when she turned on the porch light. She had leaned against me in the kitchen last New Year's Eve, her full weight pinning me to the dishwasher, telling me she could show me how to dance the Silverado two-step.

When I shook hands with the man I could feel the weight of the steel dragging down one side of my jacket. I didn't catch the man's name, and I didn't ask him to repeat it. Mrs. Newport kept a string of these guys around, phone numbers and business cards held to the fridge with poodle dog magnets.

Earl strode up the middle of Bella Vista Avenue with a liter bottle of grape soda. He was a perfect example of why I had dropped out of school, as he stopped to take a long drink and then belched almost musically, a clown even when he was alone.

My eyeballs felt like they had been soaked in Clorox. I liked Earl, in a way, but I didn't want to talk to him.

"Were you just in the Mini Mart?" I asked, working up to the subject obliquely, the way Bea does.

"No, I just found this lying around somewhere," said Earl, his way of saying: dumb question.

"You're not hurt, are you, Earl?" I heard myself ask. Maybe I was trying to wish a little pain on him.

"Of course I'm hurt," he said. He handed me the half-empty soda and I took a swig, that ripe, delicious fake grape. "Right here, on my left butt," he was saying. Hoover High had an entire student body like this. I felt years older than any of them, although I wasn't.

"The cops should take down license plates," said Earl. "Don't you think?"

The way he asked showed how my status had changed since I got up out of Junior English one afternoon, in the middle of a test on *The Scarlet Letter,* an essay exam, the changing role of the scaffold in the novel. I had put the test on Mr. Kann's desk, not meeting his eyes, turning back to give him a look when I reached the door.

Mr. Kann was holding up a yellow hall pass, not being unfriendly, reminding me that I would need permission to leave the classroom. I looked back and shrugged. It was the shrug I regretted. If I had it to do over again, I would just keep my eyes level, open the door, and walk out.

I liked Mr. Kann, and I usually enjoyed reading. But ever since my best friend, Perry Sheridan, moved to Seattle, school had lost a lot of its flavor. When I had the trouble with Mrs. Hean in World History I decided to quit. I straggled on for another few weeks, but it was a death march, class after class without really seeing or hearing.

"The cops should drive up to Rodeo and Hercules," Earl was adding, making his voice full of ridicule as he mentioned the refinery towns, as though their names weren't silly enough already. "Kick in some doors."

I finally asked what I really wanted to know. "You didn't see Bea, did you? Or did she get stomped to death in the stampede?"

"A hundred people got stomped to death," he said, emphasizing *hundred,* as though giving me news any fool would know.

"I didn't see any ambulances," I said.

Earl gave a little whinny, finding my remark humorous.

A cat slipped from the shadows and hesitated at the curb, startled by the sound of our voices.

THREE

Bea was sitting on the curb in front of my house, her cap off, her head small and round. It made me pause, how delicate she looked with her new hairstyle. She pulled the cap back on when my shadow fell over her. Her new hairdo was an attempt to compete with her mom's full-color good looks, a stab at finding a style of her own.

"Your mom was worried about you," I said.

I had never told Bea about her mom's moment of over-friendliness with me on New Year's Eve. I considered it one of those things that happen over the holidays that you try not to carry with you into the new year.

"Aren't you a little warm?" Bea asked. Bea must have noticed the way I kept my arm stiff over my jacket pocket. I ignored her, pinching the end of her knit cap and pulling it off in little jerks.

I wished I hadn't. She hung her head and examined the residue left by the street sweeper. She sat there pressing her foot

11

into the thin layer of dried silt left by the machine that careened up and down the street on the first Tuesday of every month. If someone left a car parked by the curb on those mornings the machine had to pass by, leaving a loop of faintly ridged dust you could see for days.

Her head was as close cut as you can get without a razor. It had the soft, burry look you want to reach out and touch. Bea was wearing a piece of jewelry, a little golden horseshoe pinned over her heart. Bea was obedient to her mother in a spiritless, mildly humorous way. Once I had asked Bea why her mother was heavily preoccupied with cowboys and cowgirls, and Bea had expressed a theory. She had said that some white people did not have much ethnic identity the way other races and cultures did, and that her mom was trying as hard as she could to come up with something resembling a folk tradition.

She said, "I had a feeling you might run off and leave me. I wasn't all that surprised."

I had nothing to say, taking a long look at the surface of the street.

I looked okay in the downstairs bathroom, except that the whites of my eyes were red, like beet juice.

My mom hates to stand still, and she's always running late. When she's home she likes to plant trees, paint the garage floor with waterproof sealant, replace the rubber washers in the pipes under the sink, running nonstop. One time I came in from a long trip delivering shower stalls to Stockton and she was in my room in a sleeveless sweatshirt, vacuuming my closet, the contents of my closet all over the room. Sometimes at seven in the morning she will decide to get the hedge trimmer out, and once she cut the electric cord in two, shorting out every light in the house. I woke up and found every lamp, the microwave, the television, dead to the world.

Mom manages a title company on Solano Avenue in Berkeley, and all her friends are manic, too. At parties they stand inches apart from each other and yell nonstop about capital gains. A title company orchestrates real estate sales and guarantees that the seller is the actual owner of the property. Mom has a computer with every house and apartment building in Alameda County.

Bea and I knew we were alone because the house was so quiet, so there was no danger of interrupting a meeting between Mom and her bookkeeper/boyfriend, Webster. Webster was a cheerful man who always had a pager clipped to his jogging pants. Somehow I knew Webster was not a replacement for my dad, but only temporary, and not likely to graduate into anything beyond the service department of my mom's life.

The house was very quiet. Ever since I had started paying rent on my room as a symbolic gesture, Mom tried to leave my room alone, but when she was in the house you knew it. She was always on the phone, managing the Western hemisphere. Sometimes I wore yellow earplugs I had bought at Payless, although I could hear her voice perfectly through a couple of slugs of sponge rubber.

Bea was sometimes dazzled by my mother, afraid Mom would have her help tear up the kitchen tile or hold a wrench while Mom ripped out the garbage disposal. Listening to Mom explain mortgage rates, sometimes Bea's eyes would meet mine and she would give me a smile with her eyes. It was something I have never seen anyone do so well—show a feeling or thought with a look.

I folded my jacket carefully and put it in a place where it did not belong, on the top shelf of my closet. Bea watched me favor the weight in the jacket, holding it in place so it wouldn't fall out, but she made no comment.

Her eyes asked me what I was hiding in the jacket, and my eyes looked right back.

A school bus in Los Angeles had run into a sanitation truck, and children were critically injured. A space probe was getting close to the planet Jupiter, and even though its main antenna was not responding to commands, the backup system was expected to creak into life. After that the anchorman said, "Meanwhile, in Oakland tonight . . ." and the story covered mainly the traffic snarls from the "fracas caused by what police are calling out-of-town visitors cruising the streets around Oakland's Lake Merritt." Tear gas was mentioned, plus three arrests for public drunkenness.

My phone rang as the news went on to sports, basketball, huge guys arguing with a ref, thrown out of the game. I picked up the phone and heard the jolly voice, a voice so confident it was like an actor pretending to be hearty. I could imagine the director saying, "You're very intelligent and very sure of yourself, a man of science."

I turned off the television with my stocking foot, popping the knob with my big toe, mouthing *Dad* to Bea's questioning glance.

"I just wanted to wish you luck." He lived in San Francisco, just across the Bay, but in a way he occupied another world entirely, always traveling to give lectures or sign books he had written.

"Confidence is the key," said my dad, a perky, gravelly voice, a voice they could use in ads, the manly optimist. People like my dad. He talks, and they listen. Even my mother gets along with him. "You know what Napoleon said about character."

"It's just a test," I said, meaning that I had taken a thousand just like it.

"Sure, but they call them *tests* for a reason," said my dad. His voice had a tone of argument running through it now. There were a lot of things he wanted to say but didn't. I had promised him that I would get the degree, that quitting high school didn't mean I would never get an education. I wouldn't admit it to anyone, but I now thought that quitting school had been a mistake, a result of my hurt pride and general feeling of pointlessness when Perry took all his books about military history and left town with his parents.

Maybe if I hadn't been so angry at Mrs. Hean I would still be in school. And if Perry hadn't moved north, and if I had been born with a different nervous system, one that didn't feel pride and anger. I wasn't a hopeless student, although I preferred articles about armor-piercing bullets, friend-or-foe identification codes, and howitzers, to *The Scarlet Letter*. Perry and I had wanted to design a tank warfare game, but our plans were interrupted when his dad got transferred, Sea/Land expanding its Seattle office. Perry's dad was a rising expert in robot off-loaders and was going to design ways to unpack ships full of bananas and cocoa butter.

"Napoleon said, 'Character is destiny,'" I heard myself say.

"What?" My dad was distracted by someone in the room with him, his second wife or his toddler son. I wondered if that babbling in the background was their three-year-old, unable to sleep. Or did Sofia, his young wife, engage in baby talk, sitting around in her nightie with a pout?

I repeated myself.

I had the books my dad had written, *Tiny Eden* and *The*

16

Armies of the Earth. He beamed at me from the back cover of *Prehistoric Future,* a man who didn't seem to get older from photograph to photograph. At some point in my childhood, he had gotten a little weather-beaten, a little bald, and then stayed that way, sometimes tanned and sometimes needing a shave, just back from Brazil or a conference in Copenhagen. Through the years his image smiled out at all of us, people who didn't know as much as he did.

"That's what he said," my dad agreed. "Hey, we're going but-terflying on the Peninsula this weekend, don't forget." He had been wanting to show me the Serra Skipper, an orange-and-white butterfly of the Hesperidae family, native to three acres of serpentine outcropping along the San Andreas Fault.

My careless attitude toward the test was a front. I had been studying every night, keeping quiet about it, English grammar and the U.S. Constitution and those workbooks, how to annihi-late the Graduate Equivalence Degree exam.

"You'll call me," he said.

Perky but commanding, the way he always is, telling me not to let him down.

FOUR

I took the dust cover off my computer while Bea sat there, the television sound turned to a murmur.

When the machine was running the screen reported that I had one message. I never knew what Perry was going to tell me. I had imagined the Northwest to be a rainy, mossy region, but Perry gave me the impression that it was a place so booming no one had time to send E-mail.

"Second day of kayak lessons," read Perry's message. "Might switch back to canoe. My coach is brain-dead."

"You ought to be used to brainless teachers," I messaged back, "having grown up in Oakland." We treated communication as Ping-Pong, pretending distance didn't exist. But our humor was getting heavy handed, and where we used to like the same movies and laugh about the gaffes announcers made on television, the tone of our E-mail was drifting.

No use waiting for Perry to reply—he would be playing

handball or renting an all-terrain vehicle. I turned off the computer. The molted husk of a scorpion, a Sculpted Centroides, resembled a living, glittering creature beside a rolled-up pair of gym socks.

Taped to a corner of the desk was a snapshot of Perry holding a model we had worked on when we were in junior high, a Fokker triplane the Germans used in World War I. Perry was smiling, wind mussing his brown hair, the oversized wooden model almost too much for one person to cradle in his arms.

"You were terrible at math a year ago, Zachary," Bea was saying, tilting her head out of habit, the way she used to keep the hair from cascading before her eyes. Hair grows about six inches a year.

And yet she was still Bea, gazing at me and thinking about me as she studied my attitude, the way I put my hands into my pants pockets and challenged her to give me any advice. She made a little questioning look: what makes you think you've mastered quadratic equations now?

"My dad wished me luck," I said. Meaning: why don't you?

Sometimes I wish I had another name. All through elementary school there were several Zack's, and in fourth grade I told my teacher to call me by my middle name, David. Notes would come home from school, David excels at soccer but needs encouragement in reading. My mother put on her padded shoulders—they were in style then, and she had a closet full of line-backer jackets—and marched off to stare down Mrs. Faber, who afterward tried not to call my name at all.

I followed Bea at a distance, out of the house, down the front yard. All that long walk down the corridor from junior English and across the parking lot no one had accosted me, no one had said good-bye, Zachary Madison, good luck with your life. I had gone to the library the next day, before I told my father, and spent a whole morning hunting down how to get a degree without finishing high school—a GED. Never pronounced like a syllable, but as individual letters.

"I'm sorry," I said. Bea. Bee. A little name—you had to smile when you said it out loud.

Of course one part of me wanted to say, "Sorry for what," in my best Earl imitation, what Mr. Kann had called stone-age nonchalance.

She turned, standing right in the place I had parked my Honda four nights ago. "Are you sure," the cops had asked, "this was where you parked it last?" Its distinctive grease stains were still there under the streetlight, a cluster of black oil spots. Bea put her face up to mine, her cheeks cold, although her lips were warm. "When is the test?" she asked.

"Nine-thirty A.M.," I said.

"I'll pick you up," she said. "About eight-thirty?"

Metal signs with the words NEIGHBORHOOD WATCH gleam from the streetlights. The signs display a pair of keen eyes looking out a window. The two cops who took my stolen car report, a man and a woman, had said this was the worst area for car thefts. Not for rape, not for robbery or murder. The rapists and murderers walk over into this green, tree-lined neighborhood when they don't have money for a cab.

"I'll just take the bus," I said.

When Bea was gone I stood listening just inside the house, wanting to be sure I didn't hear my mother's Volvo humming up the drive. I slipped back into my room and carefully withdrew my jacket from the top shelf of the closet.

I braced my feelings for disappointment. It would turn out to be a toy or a replica fit only to be mounted on a wall.

It was flat black, no shine to the metal. The hammer and grip were crosshatched with a fine, rough no-slip surface. I held it flat in my hand, afraid of it. I kept myself thinking, talking inwardly, sure that this wasn't a real gun. It had to be a stage prop.

The barrel was not filled in like a starting pistol, and the chambers of the cylinder were occupied. This was a loaded gun, a revolver with six bullets. I put it down gently on the top of my desk and stepped back. I read about weapons in magazines, and once my dad and I had gone to a gun club in Fremont with a friend showing off his new Colt Python. I remembered having no trouble placing shots in the middle of the white paper target.

A .38. The thing lay beside the gym sock and the computer. From my place beside the closet door I could see a scuff on the wooden grip, where the harsh asphalt had abraded the walnut stain. If the gun went off now it would blow the pillow all over the room.

When I was in first grade my dad brought home an ant farm. We set it up in the dining-room window. In those days my mother and my father were already beginning to retire their marriage, my dad spending two or three weekends a month away from home, most of the summer in the field, working hard on his first book, the one that had made his name.

The little reddish insects hollowed out tunnels, a lace of empty space, sunlight or darkness, that stretched down through the sandy earth. The bread crumbs I sprinkled into their world, the eyedropper of water, allowed them to thrive, manipulating the boulders of food down the shafts of their city.

Sometimes at night, if I could not sleep, I imagined a city underground, a human city, its many galleries harboring rest and play, stairways ever deeper, into greater and greater safety. Sometimes during the day I sketched these tunnels, the chambers for food, the halls for sports, the deepest, most secure rooms for slumber.

I didn't know where to hide the weapon. I slipped the gun into the bottom drawer of my dresser, with old drawings and school reports: "The Vanishing Mayan Cities of the Yucatan," "Pioneers of Flight." Then, very carefully, I withdrew it and covered it artfully with shoes in the bottom of my closet.

I undressed and pulled on my pajamas, but I knew I couldn't sleep with it in the room. I didn't even want to turn off the light.

What if tonight Mom came home with paint rollers and gallons of Navajo Sunrise latex she had won at a raffle, like the time three months before. What if she started to paint the house, the radio blasting All Oldies at two A.M., only this time I wouldn't have to put up with it.

I wouldn't have to go out and turn off the radio and stand in my pajamas waiting for her to get done yelling, spots of off-white all over her face.

I might forget myself, and lose control.

Or maybe she would find it first, like the time she had found the cigarette paper in my wallet, all flat and wrinkled from being sat on for months. She said she wasn't going to be one of those mothers who went into denial, and began to dismantle my room, underwear and old shoes all over the place, wrecking my wasps' nest.

I took my pajamas off and climbed into my weathered Levis and an Oakland Raiders T-shirt so old the pirate was flaking off.

Listening all the while for my mother's car, I took a jar of Vaseline down from her medicine cabinet. I slathered the gun with petroleum jelly, so the cylinder was thick with it, the SMITH & WESSON on the barrel impossible to see. I held my breath when I coated the trigger and the hammer gently, very gently.

When the gun was encased in half a jar of gunk, I settled it into a plastic Safeway bag, a few green pearls of broccoli at the bottom. The Safeway *S* got stretched out of shape, but the plastic held. I washed my hands very carefully at the kitchen sink, a thorough job, using Palmolive dish soap and hot water.

The back lawn was wet with dew, the grass squeaking under my unlaced shoes. The night was windless. The leaves of my bean garden hung motionless, the ground still moist where I had watered the Kentucky blue wonders that morning. I rummaged for a spade in the toolshed, beside the sack of lawn nutrient my mother had been spreading all over in the middle of the night the week before. I dug a hole, listening for my mother's car from time to time, hearing only the night sounds, the far-off murmur of the freeway.

I buried the gun in the backyard, beside the lime tree.

FIVE

Sleep hits me hard, a fact that embarrasses me sometimes. I sleep through operatic windstorms, hail, and even once when a neighbor was arrested one Fourth of July for firing clip after clip from his M-16.

I tugged the earphones out from under the bed, a feat of great skill for someone as sleep-sodden as I was, The Human Jellyfish Grows Fingers. I listened to a CD Bea had loaned me, by a blind man who had been dead sixty years. Bea likes this, tapes of early Hawaiian folk music, Cajun yodel-masters, the bagpipes of the Isle of Skye. I had the feeling Bea could teach me a lot about music. The guitarist was pictured on the cover of the CD. One of the guitar strings had broken and hung like a long silver hair off the neck of the instrument. His lips were parted in song, and his eyes had that empty gaze of blind people, eyes like fingertips.

When I woke again I was late.

———

Her briefcase was spread all over the dining-room table, folders and multiple listing books, little photos of houses for sale, her business cards, FLORENCE MADISON, with a tiny photo of her smiling face before she let her hair grow long. Her maiden name had been Gant, but she was convinced Dad's last name sounded better. Escrow folders had spilled onto the floor, confidential financial reports, loan applications, credit ratings. My mother could find out who owned any property in Alameda County by tapping her Social Security number plus a three-digit code into the computer in her home office, a cluttered hideaway just off the dining room.

I didn't bother being extra quiet; I had no time for that. An empty bottle of Bacardi rum glittered beside the toaster. I shook up a plastic bottle of fresh-squeezed orange juice, mostly pulp after a week in the fridge. I thought I heard Mom call my name, but when I paused, toothbrush stuffed into my mouth, all I heard was a neighbor kid yelling at another neighbor kid somewhere in the distance.

Laney College is an orderly assembly of buildings beside an estuary of ducks and a few spindly reeds. There is almost always a hot-dog stand—a cart on wheels and a man who will nab a wiener off a rotating grill with a pair of pincers. You can wander around the campus and never get the idea it is a school. The office windows have been treated with a gray tint so when you peer in to see what is going on inside, you see yourself hunching in to take a look. Even when you see something, it's a box of paper clips or a computer and an empty desk. You never see anyone reading or punching away at a keyboard.

This morning the campus was vacant, entirely, like during a bomb threat. The hot-dog stand was double-chained to a lamp-post, padlocked shut. The GED exam was scheduled to be held in the cafeteria. I was there five minutes early, but the room was empty, vending machines of canned fruit juice and sandwiches against a far wall, tables ready for people, folding chairs ready, but no one around. The clock on the wall was the same size as a clock in a much smaller room, an ordinary black-and-white classroom clock looking tiny over the EXIT.

The chalkboard, one of those brown boards in a wooden frame on wheels, had printed on it, neatly and so small it was hard to read: GED TEST IN ROOM 111. BRING PHOTO ID.

I ran upstairs, passing door after door with no number, Computer Room, Counseling Department, Financial Assistance. This was a nightmare campus, ready for business, but all the human beings gone. I stood outside a door marked SECURITY and jiggled the doorknob. I thought I heard noises from within, but they were sleepy noises, someone rousing, stretching, wondering if that pounding was coming from the door.

"Room one-one-one," said a campus cop when the door finally opened up. I had asked for room one-eleven, but the cop made it a little game, saying the three ones again. "You have to be in one-one-one in two minutes," he said.

"I'm afraid I got a little lost," I said.

He took me by the arm and stretched out a hand, a crooked finger pointing.

"But," he said, "you better move." He said *move* in a way that stretched out the word and indicated how impossible it was.

I made it to the room just as a box of exams was being opened, shipping tape torn off a box stamped CALIF. STATE DEPT. OF ED. I handed over my driver's license, out of breath. I counted out the money I had kept in a special compartment of my wallet.

People lounged, chewing gum or fingernails. Someone read a sports section, someone plucked at a tangle of earphone wires, in no hurry, the knot a kind of hobby. My dad had called up and made the arrangements, letting me take the test with a group of people who were older than I was, a couple of them much older, heavy, gray-haired men. The myth about the GED test was that convicts took it in prison, and ex-cons, trying to get jobs in barber college and bartender school. The room was mostly men, picking pimples, sucking hangnails.

It was a little like the time I was arrested and watched my fingers being rolled on the black gooey ink and rolled again over the space on a white card, each fingerprint spread out wide and flat. The room had that same stillness, another planet, a system that felt no love.

I sat in the front, far from the door, where I could stare into a corner. A little empty bracket gleamed at one edge of the chalk-board, where an American flag was supposed to be.

"I am your test administrator for today," said a tall woman with a gold jacket and gold pants, round hoop earrings. She had dark hair pulled back in a frilly little bun and caramel colored skin, hot pink lipstick like a road flare. She said she would like to welcome each one of us and wish us a very good morning. She acted like someone who had been flown in from some more stylish city to watch us all fail.

We took a few moments to squint at the pencil points or straighten the test sheet on the desk, like putting a place mat out for dinner. "You may begin when I say, 'Start,'" said the woman in gold. I caught her eye and she gave me a smile. People can be nice at the strangest times, giving someone about to be booked for assault a paper towel so he can wipe the ink off his fingers.

The volume of a cylinder equals the square of the radius times pi times height. The volume of a cone equals one-third the square of the radius of the base times pi times height. Take any number away and you have that other number that is always there, wait-ing, the blank eye that never closes, zero.

When I was in third grade, I told my fellow students that the woman who invented math had been killed in a fire. It was a good thing, I said, because she was putting the finishing touches on something even worse than math, something the schools were aching to get their hands on.

In the exam I was taking that morning, silos had to be filled with rice. Rocket fuel had been depleted by so much per minute over so many kilometers per hour. Gravel had been delivered by the cubic meter to be distributed over a parking lot that was so many square meters, over so wide a distance that I skipped the problem intending to go back to it later. Rivers flowed so much per second over dams, the basic rules of math right there for me to show off my knowledge, number added to an unknown, an unknown in a fraction, numbers with exponents. A,b,c,d. Or none of the above.

The written part of the exam was on a lined sheet. At the top of the sheet was a blank for my Social Security number. *Write an essay of two hundred words.* The back of the sheet was labeled, down at the bottom, under For Official Use Only: Reader Number One, Reader Number Two, with spaces for the readers to score the paper.

Various people have a strong influence, positive or negative, on our development. Describe such a person and explain how this person had an influence on your life.

Who makes up these tests?

S|IX _____

It took fifteen minutes from the campus to my job, a brisk half-sprint across railroad tracks, past warehouses, trucks reversing up to shipping bays, air brakes gasping.

When I saw Chief he was throwing a tarp over the back of his truck. The gray canvas was navy surplus, ALAMEDA NAVAL SHIP-YARD in faded black stenciling. The new yellow nylon rope squeaked as he tugged it through the grommets, green brass holes along the border of the stiff cloth.

Chief gave me a look of exaggerated surprise. "The crowd goes wild," he said in a sports-announcer voice.

I gave a little wave to the invisible crowd, a superstar too cool to show any feeling.

"You're early," he said, dropping his voice, implying some-thing, not wanting to come out and say it.

I stepped in beside him and tied an ordinary slipknot. This new yellow rope was slick, like lizard skin; it was hard to get a grip. The loading dock of Outlet Spa was empty, a wooden shelf like a theater stage. The shipping area was crushed white rock, like the gravel in the exam. Morning clouds were burning off, leaving the air silver and hot.

"You should use all the time they give you," he said.

Outlet Spa is in the warehouse district, several blocks west of Laney College, but another world, brick buildings with trucks backed up to the empty shipping bays, cranes and shipping containers, wooden shipping stacked among weeds. Chief swung up into the cab. He slammed the door of the GM truck and a little more paint sifted down from the rust scrape in the side.

He found the ignition without looking. "Since you're here," he said. Despite his casual manner, he had deliveries in far flung reaches of Northern California for the next week, and I knew if I didn't show up, Chief would hire someone else.

"I have to punch in," I said.

"I'll sign you in tonight," he said. "I'm hungry."

I walked into the office just to prove something, and then I couldn't find my time card in the slot with all the Ms, hardly anyone else working on Saturday. The office was empty, desks overflowing, a computer left on, bright blues and greens, amount payable blinking in the lower right. I leaned over to one of the bookkeeping department's phones. I called my dad's number and I got his machine, his wife sounding breathless and sexy, sorry they weren't in.

It was noon. The traffic was light. Chief shifted gear with difficulty up the on-ramp, the clutch having one of its bad days. The cab smelled of old iron and crankcase oil, the black vinyl seats crisscrossed with silvery duct tape. We both stared ahead through the bug-dotted windshield, a ghost-gray cabbage butterfly, what was left of him, fluttering under a windshield wiper. The rest was grasshoppers, order Orthoptera, undifferentiated wreckage, except for a tiny scrap of Painted Lady, a pretty variety of butterfly, one of my favorites, next to his AAA sticker.

"I bet you didn't double-check your answers," he said.

Chief's real first name was Bernard, and I had assumed his nickname had been awarded him because of the independent bounce in his stride, a tribe of one. He had tried to tear down my image of him, told me his name had been a family joke because he was "the chief complainer" when any rule was invoked, bedtime, bath time, time to go to church.

He had nagged at me, telling me how he regretted dropping out of school in San Diego, thinking he was going to be a roadie for rock groups, the Ice Capades, because he had a friend who did the lights for Disney on Ice. He had been driving a truck of one sort or another for fifteen years. His encouragement regarding the GED test was generally indirect, challenging: "I bet you'll get diarrhea that morning, not even show up."

"This is a rich family," I said. "The family we're delivering to." He took the clipboard from between us, the bill of lading addressed to a site in Napa.

"You aren't going to tell me how you studied all night, making sure you knew the U.S. presidents backwards."

"A Saturday delivery, the 9910 Turbo." That was the top of the line, coral pink, seating twelve people, three-speed jet action to ease pain in the lower back. "They'll give us a tip."

Chief was bouncing around behind the steering wheel, a short man, having trouble sometimes manhandling the truck despite his experience. He was used to me, and he knew I didn't like to tell everything right away.

We chose a booth, red vinyl seats you slid across all the way to vinyl padding on the wall. Except the seats weren't red anymore, dark around the edges. The surface of each table was designed to look like marble, shadowy veins, all the tables identical.

I asked Chief if he had watched the news last night.

"Harriet won't let me watch the news," he said, yanking paper napkins out of the dispenser. I didn't know if his remark meant that Chief and his wife had a sizzling sex life, or whether she just hated television. He rarely mentioned his wife, preferring to talk about his days playing softball, the time he drove a truck for a skateboard company, how he got a commission because he always sold extra boards.

"There was some trouble with those kids from Hercules. The ones who cruise the lake, looking for a fight." I said this with my voice rising at the end of each sentence, like a question, encouraging him to ask. Maybe I wanted to brag a little, how we had protected the pride of Oakland.

He gave me a look, a little ribbon of lettuce on his chin, full of some kind of good feeling that had nothing to do with me. In a previous life he must have been a very eager dog, or an otter, always at play. But his smile faded. "You walked out of that test, didn't you?" he said.

"I think you wish I did, so you can needle me."

"It's not funny."

Even when I had stood there in the bookkeeping office, my lips parted to leave a message for my dad, I just couldn't do it; I couldn't talk. Sometimes I can't shut up.

Chief had ordered both of us liverwurst on wheat berry, no onions. I paid attention to what I was eating for a second, liver-flavored glue.

"At least," I said, "I don't walk around with a dog-sex tattoo on my arm."

This was maybe going too far. Chief kept his sleeves rolled down over that fading artwork on his arm, even on a warm day. He gave me a wink—score one for me—but I could tell I had hurt his pride. Even his glasses had a knocked-together quality, the frame held together with black electricians' tape. The adhesive tape was fraying, getting hairy along the edges.

Chief carried a bowie knife thonged against his right leg. Here at this roadside place beside Interstate 80, the Chinese people who rolled the utensils in paper napkins and counted out our change were used to him. Sometimes in coffee shops up and down the state a police officer stopped and asked him about his knife, in friendly, cop way.

Cops don't start out *You are now under arrest.* They act friendly; *Whoa, party's over.* It wasn't against any law to carry a nine-inch blade against your leg, a tool of his trade, a sharp edge to cut through cardboard and packing straps.

It was the knife that had caught my eye months ago when I was looking for work, in and out of factories, laid off for the second time in a year. I filled out five or six applications a day, able to write my previous employer as a reference. I was never fired—there just wasn't enough entry-level work. I saw this man who needed a shave, scampering up and down the loading dock, a happy buccaneer. I wanted to work with that guy, I thought. I wanted to *be* that guy, armed and ready.

Later that day I was able to tell my dad that I had a new job, better than the one at Garden World. All Dad had to do was talk Mom into signing some waivers so Outlet Spa couldn't be sued if I dislocated a gut carrying fiberglass hot tubs.

I still liked Chief, but not as much as I used to. I pointed to his plaid shirt, where the shred of lettuce had fallen. He brushed it off.

"What did you do," he continued, "storm out—How dare you ask me questions like that. Or did you saunter out, like this?" He cocked his shoulders without getting up, an arrogant look on his face exactly the way I wish I had looked leaving Mr. Kann's class.

I ignored him, like my mom looked when someone farted.

It was late that afternoon when I got home and saw my mom's note under the Federal Title Company magnet, a plastic outline shaped like the United States. Her writing is all slashes, the dots on the i's sideways lines like cartoon characters showing surprise. *Good news! Call Sgt. Hollingsworth.*

Sometimes I can't do something right away—unwrap a present, answer a phone. It drives people crazy. *Why is he taking so long?* I knew what my mom's note meant. I was excited. But I had to take some time.

First I called my dad's number and got his sex-kitten wife on the machine again. The message light was blinking, other messages, other news. I paid no attention, sure they had nothing to do with me.

SEVEN

I waited at the curb late that afternoon, believing that this was the beginning of my new luck.

I knew my dad felt the same way sometimes, superstitious in little ways, wearing his argyle socks to the taping of his PBS pilot, the one based on *Prehistoric Future*. Every day under his creased gray slacks or his khaki field pants he wore those knee-high canary-and-purple socks, a gift from me when I was in second grade and thought they were really handsome.

He washed them every night, and in the thick fishbowl glass of the dryer we could see them darting and pausing, getting ready for the next day's round of good fortune. My parents never bickered and bitched at each other, even when their own personal *Titanic* listed and began to go down. We could all still make jokes about things, how the wool-blend socks were wearing out, how we hoped Dad's big toe didn't ask to be listed in the credits.

Rhonda Newport swerved over to the curb. I trotted along-side the van, wrenching open the door, piling in, as the van kept moving like a getaway car. The van smelled like spearmint, Mrs. Newport chewing gum, snapping it between her teeth.

She floored the accelerator, the van lurching around corners. We squealed way out into the far lane as we entered Park Boule-vard, cars ahead of us slowing down, easing to the side to let this madwoman and her passenger get by. I hung on to the armrest.

"I'm running on empty," she sang out.

I would later remember each detail, how happy I was. I wasn't even very annoyed with Bea's mom for being almost out of gas.

You pay in advance in most gas stations in Oakland, and Mrs. Newport gave me several wrinkled bills without paying much attention, as though money didn't matter.

Money has a dark, vegetable odor, not like the overpower-ing, breath-punishing smell of Chevron unleaded. I couldn't help feeling impatient with how slowly everything moved. Gasoline flows into a big empty tank with a noise that can be calming, a river falling softly over a dam. Some of the fuel spat-tered onto the pavement, and the gas gun would not hook back where it belonged. Mrs. Newport stayed in the front seat, hang-ing her arm down the side, dancing her short nubby chewed-off fingernails against the car door.

"Did they say what shape it was in?" she shouted over the music, KSAN turned up so loud screwheads vibrated throughout the car, music impossible to distinguish, a bellowing country-western voice.

"They close in eight minutes," I said, hanging on. I wanted to ask Mrs. Newport how she felt about Bea's new haircut, but not right now. Sometimes I could see through Rhonda Newport's shiny manner and see another person. A bright metal hair clip she must have forgotten about dangled over one ear as she drove.

She turned knobs, got the radio to shut up. "Where'd they find it?"

My mom was running a meeting in her office, the One Two Threes of Escrow, a must for new staff. Bea was in her exercise class, a martial arts and dance class combined. We were speeding along in a van I had never ridden in before, a vehicle with calico curtains and a little kitchen stove in the back. We were moving at thirty miles an hour over the limit along Lakeshore, the lake calm and empty, little black charred places in the street, like cigarette burns, last night's flares.

Mrs. Newport had that come-as-you-are look of someone interrupted in the middle of Saturday afternoon, an oversized man's shirt unbuttoned halfway down, lipstick stabbed on too fast, too bright. It struck me that maybe she was one of those women who didn't mind getting pulled over for speeding, a chance to flirt her way out of a ticket.

I pointed to the side of my head, over my ear.

"What?" she asked.

I pointed again, widening my eyes a little. She plucked the hair clip from her hair and tossed it onto the dash, where it landed in a beanbag ashtray.

Cars were jammed under the freeway, parked derelicts, abandoned heaps, the sounds of traffic overhead. It was not the rushing, windy symphony of highway traffic from down there. Trucks hit the seams of the roadway above with a metallic bang that echoed in this dark, dusty refuge for unclaimed autos.

The woman in the office had given me a form, the words *Press hard you are making five copies* prominent at the top of the page. A man in a navy-blue OPD jacket and the gray, comfy overalls of a parking attendant led us along past the rows of cars, yellow crayon on the windshields, dates, last names, and symbols that meant nothing to me, police algebra.

"All rightie," said the parking lot cop. "All rightie, all rightie," a little unmusical song to himself.

"I picked up a twenty-dollar tip today," I said.

I felt immediately foolish, bragging about my exploits in the trucking business with Mrs. Newport. She consulted for the mar-

keting division of Pacific Bell, selling people extra phone lines
for their computers and their fax machines, speaker phones and
phones that allowed you to do banking, how much money you
were down to flashing on and off on the screen.

"Twenty dollars, my heavens," said Rhonda Newport, looking away from me, kicking a chrome bumper, a little tap with her
snakeskin cowboy boot.

But it had been an interesting day, the tarp blowing half off
on Highway 29, Chief's knots failing, not mine. Then, after we
sweated all the way up to a big hole in a lawn and waited there,
holding the big, blue spa shell, a man who looked exactly like
Abraham Lincoln, but tanned and wearing a bikini brief, asked
us to stand like that while he took our picture.

"A dark blue Honda," said the parking lot cop.

"This empty space in the dash," said the parking cop. "That
mean they took something out, or was that always there?"

A hole, a red wire, a yellow wire. "They took my CD player,"
I said.

"That's a shame," said Mrs. Newport.

"It was a terrible stereo," I said. "A Pioneer FM/CD combo
that only got about half the stations, Radio Shack speakers." My
dad had bought the car from the stepson of a friend, and gave it
to me one Christmas, "just to give you a start," he had said.

"Look, they left the speakers right where they were," I was

saying, my voice dazed with the wonder of it. The gray speakers were composed of matching metal grills covered with a gray, fuzzy fabric, one speaker in each door. I felt embarrassed. For a moment I was hot with gratitude, almost tearful. My car had come back to me. Through the windshield I could read the scraggly backwards writing, my last name and today's date.

But I knew the engine would not start. That would be too much to ask. I almost wished there was some way I could contact the thieves, to thank them for leaving my car almost entirely intact. I fitted the key into the ignition.

EIGHT

I had to sign one more form, with a pen attached to the clipboard by a beaded chain. I pressed so firmly the clipboard nearly tumbled from my hands, and I had to rest it on the roof of the Honda while I finished *Madison.*

"You may now," announced the parking cop cheerfully, tearing perforated paper into separate sheets, "at this time, take possession of your vehicle."

I thanked him. He handed me the last sheet, my signature so dim I could hardly see it. Something somewhere made an insistent chirping sound, a happy electronic noise almost lost in the banging and sighing of traffic overhead. Rhonda Newport pawed through her purse, a wispy white tissue tumbling to the ground.

She held a telephone to her ear, briefly. "It's for you."

The traffic at the Bay Bridge toll plaza tends to back up. Brake lights everywhere, nothing moving. Rhonda was right: I wouldn't have been able to drive, feeling the way I did. No, that wasn't quite the case. I could have driven to San Francisco alone, fighting traffic in my Honda, but it wouldn't be right to let me do it by myself, not now. People owe some things to each other.

I had to admire the way Rhonda whipped the van from one lane to another, leaning on the horn. A dotted arrow on a Caltrans truck was directing traffic to merge to the left.

"It's not as bad as they think it is," I said. Or maybe I didn't actually say the words. Maybe I just kept repeating them over and over in my head.

The horn had a solemn, muted quality, sounding from somewhere down below our feet. I hated the way it sounded, too soft. "UC Medical Center," said Rhonda, talking mostly to herself. "I think I know how to get there."

"You *think*," I heard myself say, unable to keep from sounding like my mother.

"Don't worry," she said.

In surgery for hours.

It was a long sundown, no fog tonight, city lights just now coming on. Rhonda held her arm out the window like a wide receiver giving a straight-arm, holding off traffic while she maneuvered into another lane.

The hair clip vibrated with the engine, a dry, buzzing sound from the beanbag ashtray. My mother's news had to be all exaggeration, something we would think about a few weeks from now, a minor incident that got blown out of all proportion. I folded my arms, feeling cold, with no sense of time passing. We had always been here on the bridge, stuck, going nowhere.

I should turn on some quiet music, the kind the dentist plays, soothing, music that gets you thinking the world isn't real. I didn't touch the radio. I just sat there, trying not to think.

It was a phrase I had heard on the news. The words had never had any special, personal meaning for me. *Condition critical.*

"You can't park there," said a very stout, tall man with a zipper jacket and a glittering badge, UNIVERSITY OF CALIFORNIA POLICE. "This is emergency vehicles only."

My legs were stiff, the shrubbery unreal, people in quiet conversation, searching their pockets for keys. How wonderfully normal it all was, a newspaper machine beside a green bin decorated with a picture, a stick figure, dotted lines showing the path of his litter into a receptacle. It was probably over already, good news. Mom didn't bother to call—she wanted to tell me in person.

The man looked me up and down, his eyes hidden behind tinted glasses, black plastic frames. "We have visitor parking in lot B across the street."

Rhonda was there beside me, then, putting her keys into her purse, and some of the telephone company executive was in her voice when she said, "I'll move the car in just a minute. We have an emergency."

The man with the badge seemed to grow taller. His whole world was full of people with emergencies.

Rhonda added, like it was easy to say, an afterthought that might help explain, just a little detail, "His father's been shot."

My mother didn't even glance at Rhonda, stepping right up to me and giving me a hug. It was a real hug, a rib-crusher.

"What happened?" I asked, my voice sounding pretty calm, although higher than usual.

My mom said, hearing what I was really saying, not just my words, "I don't believe it either."

"Are they still . . ." My voice did one of its fade-outs. I couldn't even complete a question: still operating?

"They wouldn't tell *us*, Zachary. You know that. We're just the ex-family." Sometimes my mother's argumentative manner drove me crazy. But now I found it familiar, the two of us sharing the same paranoia. It was just a tradition with her, sounding relaxed and pissed-off at the same time.

"Did it happen downtown?" said Rhonda.

I winced inwardly. You had to use irony with my mother, sarcasm, adopt my mother's tone. My Mom gave Rhonda a look now, her face dead. "No," she said. Then, deciding to communicate to me, if not to Rhonda, she added, "Nineteenth Street. In an ordinary neighborhood, not far from Golden Gate Park. He stopped at a red light."

"In broad daylight," said Rhonda.

Again, Rhonda's style was all wrong, her eyes full of feeling. "Right after late lunch at his favorite restaurant," said my mom.

John's Grill, I thought. Dad liked the mashed potatoes there; he was one of those guys who never gain much weight. Right about the time Chief had been showing the man in the bikini bathing suit how to focus his Leica so he could take our picture delivering his brand-new spa.

"A car-jacking," said Rhonda, plainly trying to fit words we had all heard on the news into what was happening.

"Robbery," said my mom, with a flip of her hand—what difference did it make. "There's a police detective in there now, along with—" She didn't want to say the name of Dad's new wife just now. She gave a little shrug. "You know everything I do."

"Did they catch whoever did it?" asked Rhonda, her voice breathy, not meaning any harm, but doing it anyway, forcing my mom to say things she wasn't ready to. Maybe Rhonda was doing it deliberately, now, forcing the answers like a newspaper reporter. She had a copy of every one of my dad's books.

"No," said my mom. "They didn't catch who did it. His car went through the intersection and ran into something."

"It's terrible, Florence," said Rhonda. My mother wasn't crazy about being named after a city in Italy. She preferred the pet names my dad used to call her. My mother acts like a person cheated by life, carrying on with humor but not expecting much. She thanked Rhonda in a tone that surprised me, gentle, dignified.

"But he's going to be all right," I said.

Mom took my hand. Her fingers were very cold. My parents had never suffered the heavy-artillery sort of divorce you hear about all the time. She was always in a hurry to get to a bank before it closed, and Dad was always off to the Yucatan or Honolulu. When he fell in love with a younger woman, Mom reacted by cutting costs at the office she managed, installing new computers, firing half the staff, and winning a seat on the Governor's Economic Task Force. I think she always imagined Dad would remarry for a third time, to her, his first wife, my mom. Maybe I even hoped it was possible in some wistful cul-de-sac of my mind. Dad had always been upbeat with Mom and me, but that was how he dealt with everything, quick to get his way.

She walked me down to look out a window, the glass cross-hatched with wire mesh so no one could break in, or out.

"How did your test go today?" she asked.

I didn't respond. She wouldn't let go of my hand.

"Zachary," she said. "The police detective is in the operating room in case your father says something." She liked saying *police detective,* two words, taking solace in the way it sounded, like there were authorities in charge.

N<small>INE</small>

"Please do call me," said Rhonda.

She was looking at my mother, but she was talking to me, not a trace of Texas in her voice.

"If there's any news," my mother said, and if you didn't know her, you would think she had not a single negative feeling in the world toward Rhonda Newport, watching as she clip-clopped toward the elevator.

Half an hour later my mom got tired of pacing, running her fingers through her tumble of red hair, and got on the phone. It was a pay phone down the hall, and I could not hear what she was saying but I could hear her voice, a lot of talk over a period of some twenty minutes. She flicked her address book like a fan, looking up at the ceiling, white tiles with tiny holes.

She marched back into the waiting room to report, "We can move him if we're not happy," she said. "Stanford, anyplace, if we aren't satisfied with the medical treatment here. There's someplace he's going to track down for me, where they grow nerves in a petri dish, somewhere in L.A."

This was vintage Mom, one of the things my dad couldn't stand—when in doubt do something, something smart, something stupid, it didn't matter.

She didn't look at me. "I called Billy Brookhurst. I had to track him down, he was all over the place." Billy Brookhurst was a white-haired lawyer, wrinkled and blind in one eye, a handicap that made him seem more shrewd than any of us. He looked at reality through an unusual pair of glasses, one lens blank white.

"It's up to Dad and Sofia," I said. "Isn't it?"

An hour later my mother came back to report, "Sofia is in intensive care with him. She's tripping over tubes." She generally called Sofia something disparaging, even crude.

I expected some change in the light, in the color of the walls, at this news, but the floor and the ceiling stayed as they were, bright, fluorescent light off every surface.

"I want to see him," I said.

My mother had new, fine lines round her eyes. The waiting room was empty except for the two of us, the old magazines, the potted serpent plant—an imitation living room. She said, "One visitor at a time," giving the words a spin, invisible quotation marks.

"Where is Intensive Care?" I asked, unable to control my voice.

She shook her head.

I couldn't talk.

"Zachary," said my mother, putting her lips close to my ear and speaking in an uncharacteristically soft voice. "Zachary," she began again. She liked my name, loved saying it.

She held my head to her shoulder, a fine, feminine tweed, heather brown, something wintry she had thrown on against the cool of San Francisco summer. "I hate hospitals, too," she said.

"The surgery was successful," said the doctor. "The initial trauma is repaired as far as possible for now, and I think we can all breathe a temporary sigh of relief at this point."

"You extracted the bullet," said my mother.

"This was a through-and-through wound," said the surgeon, without stopping to choose the words, ready for the next question.

He looked like he could have been my dad's brother, a little younger than my father, but with the same high forehead, one of those people so intelligent they look handsome even when they are bone tired. My mother is not tall, and when she is insistent, she stands right in front of a person and looks up.

"Of course, I have to caution you," he said, trying to buy time with a little extra conversation, avoiding questions about sutures and disinfectant.

I could tell what my mother was thinking: Why *of course?*

The doctor said, "He is not, for example, breathing on his own."

For example.

"When you have major damage like this we have to be willing to give everything a little time," said the doctor. "He's not conscious yet," he added.

"Where, exactly, was he shot?" I heard myself ask in a kind voice, gentle, being nice to this man. I felt that I had to be especially sweet-tempered toward this surgeon and avoid hurting his feelings in any way, as though I had some power over him.

"In the neck," said Dr. Monrovia, shaking his head a little as he said it, hating having to report such a thing. He touched his forefinger to a place below his ear, just above his collar.

"The perpetrator," said my mother, gathering her strength to say this, "put a gun up to him at an intersection. And—" She couldn't say *shot him*.

I had a bad taste in my mouth, like after I've run to catch a bus and missed it, and kept running, all the way to the next stop—an attempt that almost never works. As slow as they look, buses are faster than people.

"The bullet shattered one of the cervical vertebrae—one of the bones of the neck," he said.

We waited, but it wasn't like any of the pauses in normal life, while a video starts or a movie begins, or while a lecturer finds the right place in the notes.

He put his hand to the back of his head, rubbing his skull, perhaps without being aware of what he was doing. "The transverse process, the spinous process—parts of the vertebra—are badly fragmented."

The scientific-sounding words would have been a comfort to my dad, but to me at that moment they sounded shocking, obscene. At the same time, they meant that he was in the hands of science, like hearing that a traveler is delayed in a foreign city, a famous, faraway place.

We could both tell that Dr. Monrovia was working up to something without being sure how to go on. I had the feeling that with most families he would simply talk, stop talking, and leave.

"The spinal cord is involved," he said.

A nurse padded across the tile floor, wearing white shoes with white soles, a tanned woman as tall as Dr. Monrovia. He turned his head and listened to her whisper, and gave a nod.

"You can go in and see him now," he said. "Both of you."

This sounded like good news, but the way he said it made me pause. Something had changed. My father's condition was not the same as it had been. We could all go see him because it didn't matter if there was one visitor or three.

TEN

Sofia met me at the door. Her eyes looked smaller than usual, her face without makeup, so she looked even younger than she was, reduced to a little, bare core of herself.

I had always seen her through my mother's eyes, a minor-league temptress and not very bright, one of my father's lab assistants when he was doing work on the internal structures of the killer bee. "Bee gonads," my mother had exclaimed. "This woman is an expert on bee dicks."

"I was thinking about calling the housekeeper," Sofia was saying, keeping her voice quiet. "I wondered if I should tell her to bring Daniel." She meant more than she was saying. Her mascara-free eyes reminded me of fragile living creatures, parameciums, transparent beings light would kill.

I turned around to consult with my mother, but she was standing off to one side, giving Sofia a civil smile, but not wanting to break into our conversation. Sofia folded her arms and allowed herself a moment of gazing at my mother, and I wondered what Sofia saw in the first Mrs. Madison, what hard feelings Sofia experienced herself. We had all avoided being in the same room together.

"I'm so glad you're here," said Sofia to my mother, to both of us.

This was not necessarily the right thing to say. It implied that we were here to assist Sofia in her difficult hour. My mother ran her fingers through her thick red hair, considering. I braced myself inwardly. It was impossible to tell by the half smile on my mother's face what she about to say to the young woman she called *Ms. Tits.*

"I'm glad we can help," said my mother, and I was warm inside, proud of her, as though she had just performed a very difficult anthem, high notes almost no one could hit. But the tension in my mother's face made her look like someone just back from the dentist, jaw numb.

It was impossible that we should be standing there uttering words like normal people on just another night. I had the feeling that both women were taking strength from me.

I was stalling, not wanting to look closely at what lay beyond us in the room. Besides, for perhaps the first time I saw my father's second wife in my own way, without my mother's own shadows-and-fog lighting. I had never seen Sofia so beautiful. She couldn't talk just now, leaning into me. I looked past her toward the bed, unable to see very well, not wanting to wait any longer, impatient to be with my father.

"What have you told Daniel?" my mother asked.

"I told him Daddy was hurt," said Sofia, standing a little more erect, challenging us to say that she had said the wrong thing.

There was nothing to see, just bright red digits, numbers on various pieces of equipment. The room was dark. But then, as I entered, it was not so dark after all.

I thought it was a mistake. I knew otherwise, but a part of my brain flashed the signal: *Wrong.* Wrong room. Wrong man.

In the bed lay a drowned, shriveled creature. His body was the homing place of colored and transparent tubes, a machine wheezing, alarm signals going off without any particular urgency, a steady *mweep mweep* nurses hurried in to silence.

A woman in a San Francisco Police Department uniform stepped from the shadows. "I want to have a long talk with you," my mother said, her voice hoarse with feeling. I could hear the challenge in her voice, but she was delaying that moment when she stood beside my father.

"You should wait to speak with Detective Unruh," said the cop.

Straps held my father. His neck was captured by large white absorbent pads, his head held firm. His face was puffed into a Halloween joke by a white air tube. It looked like my father was

57

committing some embarrassing sex act, fellatio with a robot, something he was doing for laughs: *How's this for grotesque, Zachary.* A tube was stuck into his nose, white tape crisscrossing his face. His hair stuck out all over a flat, white pillow.

He was naked under a thin brown blanket, exposed down to his navel, and beyond, skinnier than I had expected. The skin of his chest and much of his face was slathered with a brown-yellow stain, and it would have been easy to believe that this was not my father at all, but some derelict they had stuck full of shunts and tubes and hooked to a machine.

"Dad?" I said, like someone just coming home, announcing himself to an empty house. I didn't think it was right for us all to crowd in, so much like a deathbed scene it might frighten him.

A machine somewhere picked up its pace, my father breathing faster or his heart pumping harder. A nurse nudged me aside, adjusting a tube. "He hears you," said my mother.

I turned to her and gestured: you talk. Maybe I felt my silence would be as reassuring as anything I could say, forestalling any panic he might feel.

Mom shook her head, a little sadly. Then, like someone about to step to the edge of a high dive, stepping to the edge, stepping off, she said, "I'm here, too, Teddy. We're all here." I wasn't sure this would reassure him, three key people in his life standing around with so much to say they could barely talk.

A nurse met my glance as she unhooked a tube and fired a syringe into the small round end of the plastic coil.

A very tall, deep-chested man with skin as dark as espresso was consulting with Dr. Monrovia. When he saw us making our way down the corridor the tall man left the doctor and hurried our way.

His hand was warm, a ridge of callouses where you get them lugging suitcases or lifting weights. He introduced himself as Detective Unruh.

Un-rue. The name didn't make sense to me, and so he spelled it out loud, a man used to doing this, patient with us. "I want you to know my heart goes out to you," he said.

My mother took a deep breath, and I was sure she was going to lose control, something about his calm authority shaking her. Left with nothing to manage she would pace, fumble for the phone in her purse, call wrong numbers, swear at whoever answered, and end up experiencing her quiet form of disintegration—chew her nails, lose weight, lace on running shoes and run for miles. I had seen it a few years ago during the divorce. On the outside she played along, a peaceful exchange of legal paperwork. Inside, in a part she hated to acknowledge and probably wished didn't exist, she was on fire.

"If there is anything I can do for each one of you," he said, in a deep, resonant voice. He looked too calm to be a detective, not suspicious enough, commanding but kind. He reminded me of Mr. Euclid, the principal of Hoover High, a man with a series of business suits in varying shades of black, off-black, charcoal black, a man who would not suspend three juniors for nearly drowning a sophomore in the B-wing lavatory.

"What are you going to do?" a voice said.

It was me, my mouth. I hated the way the detective put his hand on my shoulder.

"You want to know who did this," said the detective.

I kept my mouth shut.

"You want to know who did this to your father, and what are we going to do about it." He took his hand away from me and decided to address his comments to Sofia. "You want us to offer reassurance that everything is being done."

Sofia nodded, like someone hearing a foreign language and almost catching the drift. My mother turned away and stared at the wall, and only Sofia gazed at him, half reassured by what she was hearing in the detective's voice.

"I need a list of the valuables he was carrying on his person," said the detective.

"We'll call the credit card companies," my mother said, almost eagerly—something to do.

"And an estimate as to how much cash," said the detective, squaring away to look at me.

"You found his wallet," I said.

"We did," said the detective.

I imagined the empty wallet, thin, a residual flabbiness because of all the credit cards someone had emptied—museum memberships, Beverages and More discount cards, American Express. My dad loved seeing his name on things.

ELEVEN

I did what Mom told me to do, leaving her in a motel and driving across the Bay Bridge to Oakland, the traffic a mess. Crews were laboring to re-engineer the bridge and enable it to survive an earthquake of 8.0 or higher on the Richter scale. This meant they had to close off lanes of traffic and stand talking while huge cranes waited, cocked and unmoving. Every time anyone tried to cross the bridge, it was the same—unpredictable. It had been a minor miracle that Rhonda had gotten me to the hospital as quickly as she had, and Mom said she wanted to be close to the hospital and not have to face the bridge if Something Happened.

When I was a little boy I would sit in the car parked in front of the house and pretend to drive. The imaginary landscape outside the car was forest, jungle, desert. The car was an armored personnel carrier, a drift of desert dust in the rearview mirror, dazzling the enemy.

Sometimes even now I liked sitting in front of the house, windows rolled all the way up, listening to the Volvo 960's sound system. The stereo had been paid for by a loan broker as a Christmas present, before Mom wore him out with her twenty-four-hour-a-day personality. But today I didn't listen to any music. I sat in the file-cabinet-gray car in the silence, not wanting to go into the empty house.

I unlocked the front door and turned on lights throughout the house, every one I passed, side lamps, floor lamps, even the lamp on the hood over the stove.

I called the hospital. A recording said that all available lines were busy. Don't think, I warned myself. Just do one thing after another, a smart zombie. When a human female spoke to me, I identified my father as Theodore Madison, the way his name appeared on the cover of his books.

It was a little annoying, this role of my mother's, Field Marshall to the World. But tonight I took some comfort in doing what she told me. It made me feel less stunned as I stood watering her crookneck squash, yellow grenades among the wandering vines. Her chives luxuriated in the darkness like fine green grass. And don't forget the pumpkins, she had cautioned, the green gourds sullen beneath the claw-shaped leaves, months away from becoming jack-o'-lanterns. And the star of the show, the tomatoes; I couldn't forget them.

Mom and I both share a joy in gardening, but her approach

is all inspiration and impulse, a hole for her chili pepper plant gouged out of the middle of the lawn, the shriveled green jalapenos abundant but out of place. Her vegetables thrived in messy rows, stuck too closely together, ropy tomato vines struggling out of a tub, green and yellow bell peppers wrestling for space. My beans were neat, long, slender stakes, each bean plant extending gracefully, climbing toward sun.

The lights from the house glittered on the water from the garden hose, the smell of the wet earth rising around me. I turned the water off tight and wound the hose into loops, the way my dad had shown me years before, *"so it's ready when you need it."*

I dragged a suitcase from the closet, a big gray top-of-the-line Samsonite with little brass padlocks on the zipper tabs and wheels on the bottom. She had checked the items off on her smart pink fingernails. Bras, two. Panties, two. That was easy, my mom's underclothes.

The rest would be tricky. She had asked for a sweater vest, the one she wore around the house, an ethnic-look Greek thing, something she wore when she trowled the dirt in her herb garden. Whatever else I brought I was supposed to remember the slip-ons she had custom made in Lahaina. She was not dressing for appearance.

I stuffed it all into the suitcase and then took it all out again and folded it as carefully as I knew how. Then I leaned against her dresser. She carried a makeup kit wherever she went, but she needed a little tube of medicine in case she got cold sores, which she always did under stress. She needed a container of saline solution for her contact lenses, in case the squeeze tube of Sensitive Eyes she always carried sprang a leak.

"And don't forget my glasses, in the top right-hand drawer," in case her contacts fell out of her eyes and got lost. And Ban roll-on, unscented, from the medicine cabinet. "And anything else you know I'll need." I found the little silver cross from her nightstand, the one her Aunt Dot had worn during the London Blitz, when a five-hundred pound bomb blew the roof off a church across the street.

I thought I heard a masculine cough in the background, a television laugh track. Ice tinkled in a drink. Rhonda has a set of cocktail glasses she picked up at the Alameda Flea Market, handpainted antique highball glasses, palm leaves, poodles.

I must have said something, because she was adding, "He was on the news. Channel Two. It wasn't the lead-off story. An Amtrak train ran over some people in Santa Maria, and that space probe they finally got to work. But I kept watching and there it was, Bay author shot."

My voice was able to get the question out, although the sound was strange, a talking dog.

"No suspects," she answered my question, a sad dash of irony in her voice, mock anchorman.

The television sound went off at that instant, somebody—maybe one of her boyfriends—listening in the distance, wondering who she was talking to.

Bea was at the front door, a tapping I could barely hear.

She looked up at me in the porch light. Somehow it was important, what she would say now, the words she would choose. The screen door was between us, a new door, replaced a few weeks before, a sheen of silver.

She had a red bandanna tied over her head, Bea the pirate. I opened the screen door to let her in and had to put my hand out to the wall, unsteady. She leaned against me and kept me there, gently pinned to the wall.

"There's no change in his condition," I said, repeating what the hospital voice had told me.

She nodded, her bandanna pressed against my chest as though she had foreseen this. For a while silence protected us. "They didn't come tonight," she said at last.

I didn't know what she was talking about.

But one of us had to talk, just to keep time moving along. That was how it seemed: that our actions, our words, were tiny but essential.

She looked up at me, trying to read my thoughts. "The

Oil-Towners. They stayed home."

All of that seemed so long ago, something that had happened to someone else. I was glad to hear about it. It was something solid to consider, a historic event that could be weighed
and argued.

"Maybe, when they had a chance to think, they realized that
it wasn't fun any more," she suggested, like someone offering a
tentative theory on the collapse of the French Revolution.

I nodded, trying to think about what she was saying. Bea and
I had once been very close, but I had felt distant from her lately.
Now I felt grateful for her—not just for her companionship but
for her odd, puzzling personality and for the fact that I didn't
have to get to know her, like the doctor, the detective, all these
strangers who were suddenly so important.

"I want you to tell your father something," she said. She had
never met my father, although she had seen him at a distance,
hurrying to his car.

I must have stared down at her with some tension in my
eyes, in my body. Bea was close to saying something rash, something that could change our luck.

"Tell him that reading *Prehistoric Future* made me cry," she
said. "Especially at the end," she said. I didn't want her to continue, but she did. "When he said that even if there were no
human beings, life would still be a miracle."

TWELVE

I found a place to park the Volvo all the way out on the street. The parking lot was full of cars with out-of-state licenses, New Jersey, Iowa.

The Golden Gate Motel on outer Geary was maybe a mile from the hospital, and it had a coffee shop and a swimming pool, heads tossing in the water like cabbages. The bleach odor of the pool drifted all the way across the parking lot, along with the sound of someone pretending to drown, spluttering, thrashing. The pool closed at ten, according to the rules under NO LIFE-GUARD ON DUTY. It was nearly eleven.

Mom was on the phone in the motel room, nodding approval as her suitcase rattled in behind me on its swivel wheels.

She hung up and said, "Dr. Monrovia ate lunch at the White House last month."

The people in the swimming pool were having a party, everyone drowning, spluttering back to life. "That's good news," I said. My voice was tense, fake-confident, but I managed to sound more or less like myself. "Dad could wake up to see the president bending over him. Should be very reassuring."

"Dr. Monrovia is very prominent," she said.

For an intelligent person, my mother falls for clichés. I have actually heard her refer to a real estate lawyer as "powerful and well-to-do."

"I called the American Express toll-free 800 number," she said. "They were very helpful," she said, almost dreamily.

"How about the other cards?"

"I took care of all of them. Even the Chevron card."

"Is there any news from the hospital?"

She didn't answer me directly, putting the white-and-green Golden Gate Motel pencil right next to the notepad, as though neatness was all that mattered. Then she tilted her head and let her eyes flick towards me: no news.

Bodies splashed, voices called, giggles, shouts.

"What did you find out about Detective Unruh?"

"I'm not worried about the detective," she said, taking a deep breath now and then, like someone battling hiccups, a sort of instinctive breathing exercise to calm herself down. "Did you pack my floss?"

I didn't answer at once. "I think there's a Walgreen's not far from here."

I picked up the telephone and was about to ask her for the hospital's phone number.

"Dr. Monrovia suggested seriously that we all get a good night's sleep," she said. "He said that if there is any change, it will come tomorrow morning. Sofia has gone home, too."

Maybe my mother had noticed it, too—how much Dr. Monrovia was like my father in appearance. "I should give her a call," I said. I was testing to see how Sofia and Mom were getting along.

"If you want," she said, in a way that made me put down the phone and look away from it. I sensed that the relationship between Mom and Sofia was not important right now, in my mom's estimation. Dad was all that mattered.

She made no move to unlatch the suitcase. "You forgot my toothbrush, too. The toothpaste. You brought me those rhinestone pumps Webster bought me as a joke and forgot the mouthwash." But she put her hand out to me, her fingers searching, patting mine: never mind what I'm saying.

"Open the suitcase and find out," I said. It was like volleyball—we had to keep the conversation in the air. "I brought you that purple thing and a pair of white gardening gloves."

That purple thing was a dress she had ordered custom made by a designer in Corona del Mar, flying down for two fittings. It had arrived looking like a grape with all the juice sucked out of it. "The shapeless look," my mother kept telling me the only time she had worn it, pacing the living room, waiting for Webster to take her to see *Madame Butterfly*. It had become a catch phrase. "If you don't shut up I'll put on that purple thing."

If you didn't know any better, you would think we were having a fight. We weren't. In a weary, amiable way, my mother and I were firing on all cylinders, getting along fine. But what we were really doing was trying to act normal, people remembering their usual roles, actors with Alzheimer's. "I forgot all about tooth stuff," I said.

"Walgreen's is closed," she said.

I used to think motels were fun, staying with my dad on collecting trips to Palm Springs for the Yucca moth and to Ashland for a new species of pine borer. I was crazy about ice, using the big metal scoops in the ice machine, filling the plastic container from the dresser, even though my dad did not drink cocktails and didn't need three pounds of ice for the glass of cold water he liked to drink before going to bed.

"I bet you forgot your own things," she said, kindly, complaining out of compassion for me. She has a way of putting a hand on her stomach when she talks and shaking her head a little, a little extra editorial spin: don't mind what I'm saying.

———

My roll-out bed was a mattress on spindly wheeled legs. The wheels squeaked. It folded out into what looked like a piece of lawn furniture, a bed for someone who wasn't committed to sleeping. It accepted my weight with a fine, wheezing steel whisper, like a screen door creaking open.

Mom had always believed Dad would drift back to her. I think she secretly continued to think of herself as Flo or Renny, Dad's pet names for her in those old days, when he had time for us. I wondered what he called Sofia.

Mom was in the bathroom, the door open a crack. She was smearing something on her face, and I could see her making expressions in the mirror, silent shrieks, fiendish grins, keeping those muscles taut.

Then she was in the room with me, leaving the bathroom water running, sitting on the bed, face goop all over her forehead, her cheeks. She did not say a thing, just sitting there.

I turned off the water in the bathroom and brought out a towel. I have no idea how people get the gunk off their faces. She took the towel but made no move to use it.

She had attended weekend seminars: Smile Your Way to Millions. She had taught classes: A Positive Attitude, Your Winning Number.

I called the hospital. The hospital voice said that she would transfer my call to the Intensive Care nursing station, and I froze. This is it, I thought. News. I sat down on the edge of the bed.

Mom saw my expression and stood up with the towel in her hands, draped so she could cover her face with it.

"Can I ask to whom I am speaking?" asked the next voice I spoke to, a male nurse or one of the detectives.

I told him I was Theodore Madison's son and gave him my name, feeling that this was the way our future would begin.

I braced myself to accept whatever he told me.

Unchanged and stable. The phrase repeated over and over in my mind.

The man behind the counter looked up as the motel office door made a sweet-sounding chime. "You better tell the people in the pool to go back to their rooms and go to bed," I said.

"Are they being noisy?" he said, soft-voiced man, muscles going to fat, as though he couldn't hear the voices, someone starting a game, *Marco* to be answered, from another part of the dark *Polo,* the kind of fun Dad and I used to have in motel pools.

THIRTEEN

"I can't go anywhere looking like this," she said, gazing in the bathroom mirror with the light off, her reflection a shadow.

We had not even tried to sleep. It was 5:03 in the morning. We had just turned off a movie about an ex-con who lived in San Francisco just before World War II, the city of the movie empty of tall office buildings, nothing but white apartment buildings and hills, and the blank Bay in the background. The man had plastic surgery so he could start a new life, but he didn't seem like someone with a new face. He encountered the people he met like someone accustomed to the muscles of his smile.

Mom did not put on what she called her Street Face, although she did brush her hair as we drove the streets. I was careful at each stoplight, some of them blinking red, too early Sunday morning for the normal red/green/yellow. She brushed her hair, finding snags, working the boar-bristle brush I had bought her for Christmas along with a matching rosewood hand mirror. She sawed the bristles through the tangles fiercely, as though she wanted it to hurt, taking a bitter satisfaction from the pain. It was dawn the way you hardly ever see it, the constellations fading in the east.

We had plenty of empty spaces to choose from. If I made up tests I wouldn't ask questions about how a bill becomes a law, or the formula for photosynthesis. I would ask Where do you like to park, under a tree or near a streetlight or out in the middle of nowhere?

The hospital was full of light. Sofia arrived just as we did, explaining that her sister had driven up from Santa Monica to stay with Daniel.

The nurses passed among us with soft steps, and when they hurried into his room it was the way people zip in to do something already planned, responding to a schedule and not to any sudden urgency.

But we did not go in to see him. We didn't even ask. We wanted to be close, but we did not want to alter the tempo of what was happening.

My mother and Sofia talked about private schools for Daniel when he was old enough, how important it was to control the amount of television he watched. Sometimes the effort of being patient with Sofia tightened my mom's lips and made her close her eyes for a moment. But what kept all of us calm now was not mutual understanding so much as very great weariness.

"I was born in a hospital, wasn't I?" I found myself asking, as though I wanted reassurance that I had some past connection with a place like this.

"Daniel was born down the hall," said Sofia. "The staff was so friendly I just couldn't believe it."

Sometimes I thought maybe my mother was right about Sofia. Sofia is always saying she just can't get over the weather or the traffic, or how she just can't believe something. For Sofia, a pleasant vacation was *really neat,* a kind person *dear.* Dad told me she had a brilliant head for statistics, the number of termite eggs per cubic meter.

"Kaiser Hospital in Oakland," said my mother, answering my question at last. "You knew that already," she said, not really chiding me, understanding: we had to keep talking. "Dr. Chung couldn't be there, so that doddering Dr. Luke talked the whole time about his new computer. 'Is that the baby's head,' I would ask, and he would say, 'hang in there,' and rattle on to the nurses about battery technology."

"I didn't have any trouble, did I," I asked. "Breathing?" Becoming alive, I meant.

She understood why I needed to know. She put out her hand, although she was sitting across the waiting room from me, touching the place where my hand would have been if I was sitting beside her.

Why can't I remember how the nurses looked? Each word they spoke was so important. But they dashed in quietly, hovered, and flashed softly out of the room.

He looked the same as he had before, a man being choked by tubes. A part of me wanted to cry out that he was worse than before, shrunken. But there was a presence to him, now, without a single movement on his part.

One eyelid struggled to open. The eyeball beneath it made a rapid-eye-movement dance. The lashes parted, dark iris glittering.

"He can hear you," said a nurse, a little inappropriately, not seeing what we saw, too busy at the foot of the bed.

"You're doing so well," said Sofia, leaning over the bed. "So fantastically well, Teddy."

His mouth was stuffed like a deep-sea diver's with the air tube. We could all see stupefied curiosity in his eye, wonderment, almost fear.

"You're in the hospital," said my mother, the just-the-facts words contradicted by the softness of her voice. "You were shot, but you're going to be all right."

I didn't feel as awkward as I had the first time. Maybe one part of me sensed that my father would remember our first visit and find the sight of us less like the vigil for someone who was not likely to survive. But why didn't I say something more articulate? Why were my words so insipid? "I'm here, too," was all I could say.

Dr. Monrovia wore new white running shoes and a zipper jacket. "Pneumonia is going to be a threat," he said. "Infections are always—" He made his hand go this way and that: you know how germs are. "But—" he added emphatically, upbeat, in a hurry to leave, meaning a great deal with one syllable.

Mom looked innocent without her makeup, her hair rust red, her face, which was naturally pink cheeked, all the more ruddy in the warm air of the hospital. The doctor could see the unasked, impatient *but what?* in her eyes.

He smiled, not looking like my father just now. My father's smile is infectious, while Dr. Monrovia smiled like someone having his picture taken, just enough to look pleasant. He said, "The crisis is over," like he was letting us in on a secret, just don't tell anyone else.

And it didn't sound like good news, the way he said it. He meant that the crisis was over, but something else wasn't. My mom and Sofia seemed to want to cooperate, smiling with wan relief. I was the one who said, "So he's going to be all right?"

"It's really out of our hands," said the doctor. It was one of those moments when an authority figure makes the appeal: remember I am a person, too. Remember I have feelings.

"He's not going to die," I said, a croaking little voice.

The doctor said, "The odds are in his favor now."

"He'll recover," I said. "He'll be the same as ever." My mother took my arm, trying to pull me away.

FOURTEEN

Detective Unruh was lifting a garment from the backseat of his Toyota Camry and carrying it to the open trunk. He stretched the robe carefully on the gray carpeting, smoothing the plastic dust covering carefully, straightening it so it covered the garment completely. I was hurrying back across the parking lot with a bag full of blueberry bagels, my mother's request, the Sunday paper wedged under my arm.

Morning sun dazzled, the sort of light that made me wish I wore sunglasses more than I do. I had approached the detective, but now I wondered if I should bother him as he fussed with the folds of the robe.

"Zachary Madison," he said, instead of hello.

Do you call a detective *mister?* I wondered. "My dad is okay," I said.

"I was just inside," he said, not smiling but delivering something with his bearing, a kindliness he could not have communicated with words. He tore two sheets from a roll of paper towels, one sheet after another, carefully.

"You're a judge," I said, nodding toward the robe under its One Hour Martinizing plastic. I meant it as a joke, but then I thought: I don't know anything about this man.

"Church," he said. My expression prompted him to add, "I sing in the choir."

I absorbed this information as though it mattered very much to me, and in a way it did. The car was a metallic blue, about the same color as my Honda, with a residue of car wax etched in around the *Camry*. The windows were smoke gray, the interior a mystery. A bumper sticker had been removed, leaving a ghost, a smidgen of glue. As I watched, the detective sprayed Windex on a bird dropping on the roof.

"I forgot it was Sunday," I said. Although my family had rarely gone to church, I was aware of religion as an activity, and I was familiar with Sunday as a day that began and ended the week, an island of relative stillness. We went to Glide Memorial in San Francisco once to hear an ex-mayor give a talk about famine in Eritrea, and one of my mother's few friends was a thin, athletic woman who as a substitute organist played Bach energetically, mangling most of the other hymns.

"My wife convinced me to take it up," he said. I was expected to say something about myself, what kind of music I liked, but instead I said, "You won't be working today."

His posture was that of a man who would be hard to knock down, his feet spread just wide enough, his body balanced squarely. He let the Windex soak into a second curlicue of bird turd for a few moments, and then he wiped it. I was caught up in watching how careful he was. Spit works, too, I wanted to tell him. It's the enzymes in human saliva. Great for dissolving bug scabs, anything.

Detective Unruh took some pleasure in having an audience. "I usually work with a partner," he said. "But she fell off a balcony."

"Chasing a perpetrator," I said, not asking, trying to get him to tell more.

"Termites and dry rot," he said. "Old Victorian three story, party time. She has herself a herniated disk and two broken legs. They are using a new improvement in surgical pins, gold electroplate. It'll be a while before she runs wind sprints again."

"That's too bad," I said.

My words surprised him a little. I was just being polite, but I was serious, too. People look at me like this sometimes, the men friendly and measuring, the women ready to flirt. People tend to like me. He was getting ready to tell me something, the words ready in his mouth.

"We have a witness," he said.

I looked at him like someone stalling, trying to remember how to spell and define *hypotenuse*. But maybe it was the faintly religious weight to the word, like people who witness for Jesus, that confused me.

He said, "A man who saw the shooting take place."

"Who?" I asked before I could think. I didn't understand why it troubled me that someone had seen it happen, but it did, my dad suddenly helpless in broad daylight.

"A merchant," said the detective.

The word sounded like something out of another century, caravans and camels, sacks of spices from the East.

"He came forward and said he saw it from beginning to end." Everything the detective was saying sounded unreal and archaic. *Came forward.*

"There was a line-up," I said, feeling far beyond my own personal experience.

"We use a line-up sometimes," he said, to let me know it wasn't an ignorant remark. "In this case we had photographs of people who have been arrested before." I could sense him simplifying for me, keeping the information smooth.

A merchant had seen this crime and done nothing. Watched it happen and not run out into the street ready to risk everything to save my father. I had to take a deep breath and lean against the car, studying the speckles of the asphalt, the different shades of gray.

"We haven't taken anyone into custody yet," said the detective, letting me absorb a little more of his cop talk.

"You're looking for someone," I said. Someone with a name, a face. The sunlight was so bright I had to close my eyes.

"Our investigation continues," he said. He said this with a little extra meaning, trying to peek out from behind the official phraseology.

"His wallet was empty, all the money gone," I said.

"They didn't leave anything of value," said the detective.

"That means my dad gave him the wallet." I tried to say this all in a rush. "Handed it to him. And he shot my dad anyway."

Detective Unruh slipped a pair of sunglasses out of his breast pocket and took a while unfolding them.

Whenever I began to think that the hospital was a regular place, a building of people engaged in ordinary activity, I would glance into a room and see a woman lying with her mouth open while a nurse tapped her arm, looking for a vein. Or a man holding his stomach like it all might come out, watching while a bag of blood was hung on a pole.

Mom fished a bagel from the crinkly paper bag.

"They'll catch him," I said.

I didn't understand the look my mother gave me, touching a bite of bagel into her mouth.

"You specifically said blueberry," I said.

The Sunday newspaper amounts to several pounds of nothing, instant recycling. A television schedule is usually slipped deep inside the real estate ads, the rest of it stories they could write weeks ahead of time, another tenant hotel closing, the crab catch at a record low. But I hunted through the bale of newsprint until I found it, four short paragraphs. The article did not give the titles of my dad's books.

My dad's prospective PBS special was never actually shown on television. It won third place in a film festival in Mill Valley, and then KQED had a major cutback. I thought of my father as famous, but once I saw a letter my dad had torn into pieces. I nudged the fragments together without actually taking them out of the trash can, not wanting to pry. "Who cares about spittle bugs?" someone had written in the margin of my dad's letter.

"I saw a priest," said Sofia.

"People die here," said Mom. Every now and then I could see Mom's eyes lose their luster and stare at Sofia in the old way. But at other times something new was developing between them.

"He was wearing his collar. He looked our way and took a step in our direction, and do you know what? I stood right in the doorway," said Sofia, as though she would be able to block the passage of any halfway determined person. My father must have been attracted to short women. "You know how Teddy detests that sort of thing."

"The priest didn't mean any harm," said Mom.

Sofia made an incredulous little laugh. "What if you were stricken—" Her word choice impressed all of us. *Stricken*. Sofia blinked, had trouble maintaining her composure, and then continued, "and you looked up and saw a priest in the doorway?"

FIFTEEN

For such a sunny person Rhonda Newport keeps her living room very dark, and even with morning light outside, I had to peer around at the framed color photos of the American West on the walls, sand dunes with sidewinder tracks, a mesa and a grazing pinto. It was Monday morning, and I felt like I was living in a rented body. I was telling Rhonda Newport what had happened to my car.

"I thought Bea could drive me down to the lot," I concluded.

"They towed it back?" she asked in a just-checking tone.

"We left it there beside the street," I said, feeling like I had to defend the cops.

"Hauled it right back, maybe fifty yards," she said, showing exaggerated exasperation, letting me know how she felt.

I knew that she was just being nice, expressing sympathy, but I had put the frustration out of my mind and I didn't want to wake it up. I had dropped by the parking space the night before, prompted by Mom when I had to admit that I had lost track of my car's actual location. At first I had been certain the vehicle had been stolen again, but the cop computer showed it right back in space 209. The lot was closed at that hour late Sunday night, and I would have to come back in the morning.

"Bea's gone," said Mrs. Newport. "She's working on the brand-new speed bag down at the Pit. One of those real tiny ones." She indicated the dimensions with her hands, the size of a child's head. "She said she was learning to patter-punch." She rolled her eyes as she said this: my daughter the pugilist.

The Volvo was parked in front of my house. I had made the long walk over to Bea's place, because if I drove down to the cop parking lot, I would be in possession of two vehicles. For the moment I wished all the cars in the universe would evaporate. I imagined my dad's Mercedes, an older E-class four-door, now totaled because the car had kept rolling for half a block, wiping out a line of parked cars before something stopped it. At least, this was how I pictured it. The cops had a witness, and he would detail what had happened.

What had stopped my father's car? The back of a truck, perhaps, or a fire hydrant, a white, gushing geyser. And Dad was so careful, waxing the car twice a year so the Turtle Wax would not build up and obscure the shine. Always wax on a cloudy day, or in the garage, he had taught me. Spread wax in bright sun and it dries too fast. He used saddle soap on the leather seats.

"You look like a young man badly in need of a waffle," Rhonda Newport said. A pink bathrobe was sashed hard around her middle, and she had done something with her hair, a pink ribbon dangling. Her moccasins made no sound on the kitchen floor.

An appliance gleamed on the kitchen counter, a stainless steel jewel box with a dial on top of the lid. She released a catch, and the hinges opened silently to expose a dark grid smelling faintly of hot cooking oil. "A wedding present," she said. "A Krup limited edition. The Rolls Royce of waffle irons."

"What a nice wedding present," I said, like someone learning of an ancient, exotic custom.

"If you bought one now it would be Teflon," she said.

I made a little face: Teflon, how awful, although I didn't know anything about it.

"I have a quart of batter in the fridge," she said, letting her hip lean into me. "And you look hungry."

She was already unpeeling the end of a half stick of Challenge butter, the wrapper uncrinkling. She sliced off a yellow segment and poked the butter down into a coffee mug. She put it into the microwave and we both watched the mug, with its hummingbird decorations illuminated in its prison, rotating on the glass turntable as the microwave clock counted down to zero.

"You didn't tell Bea I was coming," I said.

"Why would I keep a secret from my own daughter, Zachary?"

Any number of reasons, I almost said, before I could think. I added, "It wasn't much of a secret."

"You could take a cab," she said. "The phone is over there, under the corn husks."

I tried to remember which bus line ran downtown, and if it still ran from up in the hills. There had been cutbacks lately. I could call AC Transit and ask. "I'm not sure I have enough cash on me," I said.

"Spoken like a gentleman," she said, painting the dark grid with a white brush she dipped into the mug. It was the kind of brush Mom used to baste turkeys, and the bristles made a soft padding whisper as the iron began to sizzle.

The corn husks were tied together at one end, a great yellow claw protecting the telephone. Rhonda Newport's tamales were admired even by my mom. They were stuffed with ground chuck and homemade tomato sauce and other ingredients you don't think of as tamale filling, white hominy and raisins.

"Get me that orange juice container out of the fridge."

"My dad is going to be okay," I said.

She gave me a look, tentative, hopeful. A little frill of nightie had wafted out of the bathrobe collar. "This is such a relief, Zachary." She had avoided asking, I realized. She was being sincere, but she was being something else, too. "I kept waking in the night tossing and turning." For some, tossing and turning is just a phrase. But I could picture Rhonda Newport punching her pillow, kicking her blankets to free them from the foot of the bed.

The container was designed for citrus, oranges and lemons. The spout and the handle of the pitcher were fuzzy, the way old plastic gets, wearing away into fine cilia. In ten thousand years it would wear out.

"Get me that ladle off the hook," she said.

She stirred the thick stuff for a moment. She scooped a glop of batter out of the pitcher and let a few coins of it dribble onto the iron. They bubbled and firmed, instantly brown. She flicked them free with a spatula and poured a small flood of batter over the griddle. It was almost like someone making a mistake on purpose, spilling a lake of plaster over a black, pristine surface.

She swung the lid shut, and the waffle iron gave off a whisper.

"You aren't having any?" I asked.

"Not me," she said, one hand around her coffee cup. The turquoise ring she wore tinkled against the handle of the cup.

The syrup had a cabin on the label. People used to eat this in earlier times, the label instructed us. The syrup was cold, so it flowed instead of splashing. It ran out through the streets and avenues of the waffle city, and I took some pleasure in watching it fill up all the even spaces.

"His spine wasn't injured," said Rhonda Newport.

"No, it was," I said. "There was some smashed bone—" I couldn't remember Dr. Monrovia's exact terminology.

Rhonda put her hand to the back of her head and parted her lips. Then she shook her head and smiled apologetically, like someone who has forgotten her question.

SIXTEEN

"What are *you* doing here?" asked Chief.

He was folding up his road map of California. The map was so old it was separating at the folds, and he pinched it together with a red plastic paper clip. Matt Espinosa, one of the assistant shipping clerks from inside the plant, was strapping on a back brace over by the loading dock, having trouble getting the worn Velcro to grip. It was a hazy morning, sky the color of milk.

I made a show of testing knots, the yellow nylon rope making a satisfying squeak with each tug.

"You don't have to work today," said Chief, refusing to look at me, like I wouldn't be officially there unless he acknowledged my presence.

It was Tuesday, after one day off from work, a day spent reading magazines and eating jello salads in the hospital cafeteria.

I opened the passenger door to the cab and climbed in. I was instantly surrounded by the smell of the old truck and the protective quiet. Matt hesitated and made a shrug: what am I supposed to do?

"A delivery schedule doesn't mean very much. At a time like this." This was not like Chief at all, grim-faced, terse little sentences. "Espinosa said he'd help me out."

"Tell Matt to go back to the shrink-wrap department."

There was nothing I could do to speed my dad's recovery, nothing I could do to help my mom and Sofia march up and down the waiting room.

Chief shrugged. Matt gave me a wave, a show of being cheerful, both of them letting me know that whatever I wanted was okay.

Chief started the engine and drove the way he never did, about three miles an hour, pea gravel crackling under the tires. He eased the truck along so slowly it nearly stalled, so he tucked the gear back into neutral, as though actually picking up some speed might disturb me.

Even on the freeway he was driving cautiously enough to get a ticket for going too slowly. He had things to say, and he didn't know how to begin. He had even forgotten to cover up his dog-sex tattoo, wearing a T-shirt that exposed the profiles of two hound dogs mating, fading blue on his upper arm. I had thought of my dad's condition as something that had happened to me

and my family, not guessing that other people would feel connected.

We drove east, out of the cool basin of the Bay Area, into in-
creasing heat. We passed hills cut in half, farms beside the freeway, houses, mops leaning on front porches, and barns, doors
open, dark interiors. The hills died out, flat land stretching in all
directions. Near Stockton we left the freeway and rolled down a
two-lane road, orchard on one side, empty nothing on the other,
pasture, weeds.

"If you get hungry, Harriet made me an extra," Chief said.

I felt the brown bag between us, rolled up tight, crammed
with what I called bug-bread sandwiches, wheat-berry bread,
bits of wheat like insect abdomens, Chief's favorite. "What is it
today?" I asked. "Bacon and peanut butter?" One of his favorites,
one bite and you couldn't talk for half an hour.

He gave a sharp little laugh: not so lucky. "Cottage cheese
and grape jelly," he said.

A construction site lay exposed in the heat, bare dirt, trucks glittering. I thought this was where we would turn in and find a
shady parking place under one of the few trees. We passed it by,
although Chief took his foot off the gas pedal to give it a look.

"You can pick up a lot of overtime working a job like that,"
said Chief.

Men walked in the air, supported by the yellow skeleton of building, bare wood.

"But there you'd be," I said.

Chief shifted gears, having trouble with the truck because of the smog device that had been repaired that morning, sucking off some of the engine's power so its exhaust would run clean.

"It just seems like a wasted life," I said.

He rolled down the window as far as it would go.

I heard myself keep talking, the Amazing Nuclear Mouth. "You spend most of your time keeping your bills of lading in alphabetical order and snipping your receipts together with that little yellow stapler."

He made a point of watching a crow abandon a telephone wire and flap over the road. For a long time his driving was a way of responding to me, his eyes shifting from the speedometer to the road to the sky, keeping us right on the speed limit.

The truck lumbered up a gravel road toward a pink stucco house, balconies hanging off every wall, a view east, west, and north of the flat, empty landscape. A man waited for us, so little happening in his life that our arrival was enough to make him stand and watch us for the last half mile, a little figure in the middle of all that heat.

An excavation showed where we were supposed to leave

the hot tub, one of the health club models, compact but heavy grade, made to last.

"The Lord has been good to me and my wife," said the tall man with white hair all over his chest. In a cowboy hat and a pair of tartan plaid shorts he looked like an ad for skin cancer, how to get it. He was already going red, a man probably sixty who needed his mother to tell him to go get a shirt.

"Beautiful out here," said Chief, the country scenery making him drop the beginning of his sentences. "Big sky, fresh air."

"Blessed us with five healthy kids and seven grandchildren to date," said the man, signing one of Chief's forms.

"They'll have fun in that hot tub," said Chief.

"Oh, this is mainly for medical reasons," said the man as he put his fingers on the line where he had signed his name, feeling the contours of his own handwriting. "Reasons of health," he elaborated, like maybe we hadn't understood what he meant. "My hips," he added.

"I hear nothing but good things from people with hip trouble," said Chief, accepting his clipboard, examining the form, making sure all the little blank spaces were scribbled in.

"Bone spurs," said the man.

"Nothing like hot water to ease the body," said Chief. He had a gift with people, agreeing with them with a smile. "Hot water and enough time to take it easy."

"Easy does it," said the man.

I couldn't stand it when grown men did this, open their mouths and fire inane statements at each other, like a contest, who can say the dumbest things.

I found a pebble in the path and gave it a kick, not able to just stand there and listen to Chief practically promise the man a cure for bone spurs, whatever they were, deteriorating calcium in the man's limbs.

SEVENTEEN

Sometimes I forgot for a few heartbeats, and it was just another day, two lanes, the sky clear, all the way to the horizon.

We rolled north along the two-lane, a drift of sprinkler mist touching me through the open window. The almond orchards were irrigated by sprinklers on high poles, white plumes of water.

"Let me know if you want to stop," Chief said.

Chief had a citizen's band radio, a veteran Magnavox with two knobs missing. I never saw him use it, and he didn't carry a phone. If I wanted to call the hospital, I would have to trek across a plain of petrified cow pies and knock on a door. "Doesn't it get on your nerves when someone says how the Lord has blessed him?"

"He was just being friendly." He looked over at me, a question in his eyes, the passing scenery reflected in his glasses.

"Thinking that God is wrapping up presents for you and you

alone," I heard myself saying. "A new house, a big new lime-green fiberglass hot tub, little skin cancers on your shoulders."

"You're just mad because he didn't give you a tip," said Chief. He worked the transmission out of fourth and into third, the gear box grumbling somewhere under our feet. Chief never complained, but I knew the old truck was a bitch.

As we slowed down something made me want to break Chief's clipboard into tiny pieces. Maybe it was the bantering Chief kept up, able to pretend things were normal. I hated him for it, but at the same time I was grateful. I had written my GED essay about Chief, the person who had influenced my life. I should have written about my father.

Chief swung the truck up onto a rutted dirt road, fighting with the steering wheel. He let the truck lurch to a stop. For a moment I thought he was going to say, That's enough out of you, Zachary, get out.

He turned off the engine, but even that was not a smooth operation. The key turned stiffly, and when the engine died the truck began to roll a little. Chief pulled on the parking brake and the truck steadied, stopping. The quiet was punctured by the sounds from under the hood, hot metal falling still, cooling. He climbed out of the truck, and I followed, up to a barbed-wire fence.

Silence. Hot wind. The *crush crush crush* of our footsteps.

"Can you believe having a head that small?" he was asking, his voice loud in all that quiet.

An ostrich peered at us from behind the fence. It had to turn its head sideways to observe us, like any bird, its head bare of feathers except for a few white hairlike filaments. Its ear was a fuzzy hole in its skull. Its feet were gray talons, huge, dinosaur prints in the dust.

"They buy these ostrich eggs for two thousand dollars each," said Chief, holding out his hands to show the size and shape. "Keep hoping a demand for ostrich enchiladas will sweep the nation."

Chief liked this, stories about people blowing their cash in a stupid investment. His father had been a pit boss in Vegas. Chief said most people were hopeless when it came to handling money, thinking they could beat the odds. But there was some kindness in his tone, too, as though people couldn't help dreaming.

A woman stepped down back steps in the distance and made her way toward wash hanging on a line. The line itself was invisible, mirage rippling the air. She saw us and smiled, the whiteness of her teeth across the distance, friendly, someone we would never know.

"Maybe they like the birds," I said. "As pets."

"Would you?" But he wanted to agree with me. I could tell

by the way he picked up a spine of weeds and held it out to the ostrich. Another bird marched from behind a shed, wending its way across the trampled earth.

As the second fowl cocked its small, dark eye, a dog scrambled from the back porch of the house. The woman called to it, but the dog ignored her, barreling across the drought-yellow lawn, swinging wide to avoid the angle of the barbed-wire fence, running hard down the road to stop right before us.

Half German shepherd and half haystack, he exposed his teeth at us and released a long, low growl. He gave us an especially ugly display, peeling back the skin of his snout, showing every single tooth.

The woman was calling, a name that sounded like Nero. I have a theory about dealing with angry dogs, and it includes speaking in a gentle voice and holding out a hand the dog can sniff. Nero stretched his neck toward my hand and barked, dog breath on my fingers. He was sour-smelling.

Each bark shook something in me, and as I began to back away Nero bristled, a ridge of hair up and down his spine. He crept after me, one step after another, an iron-edged growl backing me toward the center of the road.

Chief wore one of his merry little smiles. "Look here, Zero," he said. He wrenched open the truck door, reached in across the seat and rummaged, bringing forth half a sandwich.

My essay had been about the time Chief broke up a fight be-

EDGE

tween two massive Tongans on the loading dock, two cousins who had just been joking around and suddenly pushed with a little too much weight. Chief had insinuated himself between the two men with a laugh.

It was the laugh, the carefree manner, that had killed the fight. "If you're going to show off your choke holds, make us buy tickets." And the time he parked the truck in a driveway in San Leandro, and a furious man stormed down at us, holding up his pants with one fist, shouting that if we left our truck there he would have us arrested. Chief agreed that sloppy parking should be punished by the firing squad, and the man ended by leading us to a pony keg of beer and saying he could nuke another plate of nachos in the microwave.

And here was Chief, offering bug bread with grape jam seeping through, cottage cheese crumbling at the edges. The dog nosed the air. Chief put the half sandwich down beside an ant colony, cinnamon brown harvester ants, a hole with a halo of ant-processed earth.

I'm glad I'm not an animal. But for a moment Chief and I were silent, enjoying the dog's pleasure. He lapped the bread, taking the sandwich apart, tossing it so he could wedge it into his jaws. He wolfed the last crust, eyeing us with little of his former aggressiveness, his tail beginning to jerk from side to side.

"Zero the Hero," said Chief.

EIGHTEEN

"Dad, you look great," I said.

For a rare instant I was alone with him, no nurse, no Mom or Sofia. I tried to convince myself that I was not lying: he looked much better.

A machine sucked in and sucked out. It was too warm in the room. My dad's face was flushed and I was sweating inside my shirt. It was Thursday afternoon, the fifth day after the shooting. A box of Swipes, white tissues like Kleenex, perched on a half table swung to one side. I touched one to his forehead, blotting moisture.

I had never done anything like this for my father. I almost expected one of us to need a joke, something to counter embarrassment. But there was no embarrassment, only his look of acknowledgment.

His eyes crinkled, asking.

"I took the test," I said, sure he wouldn't remember. The memory of the previous Saturday morning was a dim historical scrap, unattached to anything happening in this room. But I meant it as an offering, good news from the ordinary world. Only as I spoke did I feel the flimsiness of the report, how little it must matter to him now.

His eyes were on mine, looking into me, full of questions. A blue tube led to a button in his throat.

The words tightened up on me, but I said them anyway. "I'm pretty sure I did okay," I said, trying to make it sound casual. I wasn't sure at all.

He blinked. The blink meant something. His eyes rolled, taking in the room.

"A lot of equipment," I said. "A busy place. A nice place," I said, giddy, eager to have even a one-sided conversation with him. I almost mentioned how hard it was to park with all the cars everywhere, as though I was making small talk about shopping downtown.

His tongue licked his lips, his lips parting, then shutting again, and I could read his eyes. When I was out in the corridor again, the bustle of hospital routine passing by, I could hear what he was thinking.

Daniel put a small plastic figure into my open palm and closed my fingers around it. The space warrior was completely hidden. I wiggled my fingers so the head of the cosmic combatant stuck out of my fist. My half-brother laughed and tried to poke the helmeted head back into my grasp.

"You don't have to draw pictures," my mother was saying. She was already starting her spell of weight loss, a new wrinkle in her cheek. Some people balloon under stress; Mom does just the opposite. After a while she starts to look worn and dry, like a long distance runner who has been pounding marathons in Death Valley.

"It helps me as much as it helps you," said Dr. Monrovia. A white, smooth surface of the drawing board squeaked as his marker added lines and arcs, chirping softly when he shaded in, cross-hatching carefully. The marker ink smelled like alcohol. "I always think better when I have something in my hand," he added, trying to disarm my mother: I'm just another person doing a difficult job.

"You draw very well," said Sofia. She was dressed in tight black pants and a full-cut flowery blouse with long, oversized sleeves, a shiny material, black and rose satin. It made her look big on top and puny below, armor that went only halfway. I found it hard to dislike Sofia now. A truce had been declared in my brain, negative thoughts piled like weapons under UN supervision.

"Red is for the spinal column," said Dr. Monrovia.

"And black represents bone," said my mother, swinging her foot, *kick kick* against nothing.

Dr. Monrovia was hard at work on the outline of the skull, blunt nose, sharp chin. "I haven't discussed this with Mr. Madison, but I will. I have a theory about the ability of patients to absorb bad news during post-trauma recovery."

"Tell me about your theory," said my mother. Not us. Me. Mom always hated a certain type of person, turning on the mute whenever a weatherman blew a line, pointed to a smiling sun and saying "in this area of severe thunderstorms."

"My views aren't exactly the issue here," said Dr. Monrovia. He looked even less like my dad today and seemed to have lost hair since I had seen him last, fluorescent lights gleaming off his scalp.

Mom looked into her purse, took out a bottle of Advil.

"People during trauma," said the doctor, "are more able to absorb bad news than people generally think. The psyche goes into crisis mode, and in this frame of mind the patient can take in bad news with a calm that would be very unusual in a healthy patient." He gave a little tilt of his head: my theory, take it or leave it.

Mom popped three of the pills, without water, like someone snapping up M & M's, swallowing with no difficulty, practiced at this sort of thing.

"Mr. Madison is recovering from surgery, fighting infection successfully, vital signs in good shape." He snapped the cap back onto a marker, and arranged the markers in a long convoy in the tray at the bottom of the drawing board. "He was in good physical condition before this event, and that's a blessing." He selected one more marker, with an air of someone putting the last, finishing touches on a work of art.

I experienced a flicker of pride. My father had always jogged, every afternoon, around San Francisco's Lake Merced, plodding along even in the drizzle. When it rained he jockeyed in place on his exercise bike, an Airgometer that sounded like a wind machine, a digital gauge counting the calories he was burning.

"He cannot breathe on his own," said the doctor. "He has no sensation in his extremities."

My mother was about to say something, and the doctor hurried himself along. "I alluded to this before," he said, sketching in the rest of the outline in blue, a profile like an ad for cough medicine, Where Colds Strike.

A dotted line stitched across the blank white, intersecting with the neck. It was a feeble drawing compared with the bullet slashes of comic books, a tender hint of real harm. "If a muscle is severed—"

I thought I could read his eyes as he considered adding more hurtful words, *torn, sliced,* and deciding against them, sticking to the brief lecture he had delivered many times, in this very room. "The muscle fiber can grow back. I think of muscle as being like wood, full of green sap, able to heal itself together again. But with our nervous system we face a different situation. In a child, or a young person, we might hope to see some re-generation—"

"He's going to be paralyzed," said my mother.

I expected the surgeon to respond: no, of course not, that's not what I'm trying to say.

He said, "We have to anticipate that."

I told myself the doctor had not spoken these words. My ears had tricked me, my brain making up voices on its own.

"How bad will it be?" my mother was asking, draining all the emotion out of her voice, like a pilot's voice during turbulence, just the words, no feeling.

But there was something relentless about her, too, needing to be in charge. I wanted to tell her to just shut up. She was making it worse.

"I'm going to have a physical therapist examine Mr. Madison tomorrow. The sooner we begin the better." He lifted a finger to beg my mother's patience. She turned away, unable to look at him.

It's hard to say what pause, what gesture, earned my trust. He spoke in a different voice, gentle, like the recording of a pleasant *The Bay Area has suffered a major earthquake*. "We have to expect the paralysis to be from the neck down, and permanent. We have to expect him never to recover normal activity."

Sofia jammed a knuckle between her teeth. My mother looked at the tip of her shoe, breathing hard. Daniel at last wrestled the space knight from my hand and wiped it on his T-shirt.

"But it's too soon to tell," said Sofia.

My mother put a hand on Sofia's sleeve and squeezed. The satin bunched in, Sofia slim under all that padding.

NINETEEN

Late Friday afternoon I plopped down in front of my computer, turned it on, and read a message from Perry. He said that his kayak coach was one of those guys with thick necks and small ears, too muscled to do anything but stand around and look strong. But Coach Bicep was an expert in grizzlies. He led expeditions into Denali National Park, and Perry might trek up there next summer to help tag bears.

This was typical of Perry, always saying something dramatic, a way of keeping our friendship going. At the same time he made me realize how far away he was, gossiping about a kayaking grizzly expert I would never meet.

I sat the keyboard for a long time, but I could not bring myself to tell him anything about my dad. I felt like a witness finding it impossible putting words to some obscene thing he was under oath to describe.

Deena's Diner was a former health food restaurant trying to look like restaurants in another era, green Depression glass saltshakers and sun-yellowed Coca-Cola ads on the walls. It even sported an awning that overhung College Avenue, EAT AT DEENA'S. in white lettering against the blue canvas.

I hadn't bothered to change out of my work clothes, heavy gray pants, steel-toed boots, a Ben Davis cotton blend shirt with the sleeves cut off. One of the nurses told me Dad had fierce headaches, the only part of his body with feeling.

Unable to tell Perry about Dad, I was in no mood to talk to anyone. I realized as soon as I sat down that my mom was right: she had taken to jogging out by the Marina in San Francisco and up the long hills into Pacific Heights, providing herself with sweatpants and a nylon zip-up top. When she was sitting still, you could hear her experimenting with breathing exercises, laboring to keep her nerves under control.

I should take up running, weight-lifting, anything. Bea pretended she didn't see me when I came in, but I could tell by the sudden pink in her cheeks, the brightness of her eyes. I found a table and leaned back, watching her deliver a plate of tuna salad littered with bean sprouts to a man sitting under a Ford hubcap on the wall.

The man smiled up at Bea, one of those men who like to look women right in the face and let them see what they are missing in life. And Bea was looking right back, hitching her hip out to one side just like her mom. The man was laughing and Bea was joining in, only Bea's laugh was quiet, like a cough.

I stretched out my feet and leaned back in my chair, a person who could take his time.

"Zachary, I didn't expect you," she said, and I was even more sorry I had come. Bea was embarrassed about her apron, I could tell without asking. And the little plastic button, HI, I'M BEA, and the other button, ASK ME WHAT'S SPECIAL.

"Is the tuna fish salad special?" I asked.

"Cobb salad is," she said in her scratchy voice.

A big woman with a broad, fleshy face leaned against the counter, watching. When she shifted her elbows, a paper clip stuck to her elbow dimples for a second.

"What is Cobb salad, exactly?" I asked.

"It's got iceberg lettuce and cubes of turkey and avocado and bacon, if you want, and grated egg, served with a pitcher of bleu cheese on the side."

"I'm pretty hungry," I said. "That doesn't sound like enough food." Bea and I used to go up to Tilden Park and toss a Frisbee around, both of us having just the right touch. We could snap a Frisbee back and forth for half an hour and almost never let it kiss the grass.

"Zachary, don't do this," she said, responding to the un-friendly weight behind my words. "Come pick me up at eight and we'll go the gym."

"And watch you box?" I knew I was being unfair to Bea, mad at myself because I couldn't explain to my best friend what had happened to Dad.

Her lips pressed together for an instant. "I work out with the big bag and the speed bag, to music. You can do it, too—I'm allowed to bring one guest on a first-time visit."

"You don't call me," I said.

"I do," said Bea. "I think about you all the time," complete with a little catch in her voice. "I leave messages."

"Why do you suppose it's called Cobb salad?" I asked.

The Big Lady eased herself around the counter and brought herself within earshot. She gathered some menus off a nearby table and stacked them, tapping the bottom edge on the tabletop. "That's a matter of some debate," said Bea, sounding like her old self, the way we used to be.

"Can I order it without the lettuce?" I said.

"Zachary, I'm going to bring it out here and dump it all over your head," said Bea, making it sound like one of those carefree things people say to each other.

"This is why I never see you. All these friendly people here in Deena's Diner." I said *Deena* especially loudly because I wanted the big woman to hear me. "Your mom doesn't hesitate." I was being unfair but I couldn't shut my mouth. "She drives right on up in that new van of hers, with the calico curtains. She asks me if there's anything else she can do."

"I don't want to hear about it," she said.

"You ought to learn how to lean forward and let your front hang all over people, just like your mom. Pour out that free refill and make the customer smile."

"I think about how much you're going through these days," said Bea, her voice broken. I shouldn't have talked about her mother.

But I couldn't stop myself. "My dad can't cough up his own phlegm and you stand around carrying on the family tradition, wiggling your butt for customers."

I had not expected to say anything like this. I knew at the time it wasn't right. Rhonda Newport's pass at me had been a nonevent, I had come to believe, the result of eggnog and "I'll Be Home for Christmas" on the stereo.

"Bea, honey, you want me to ask this gentleman to leave?" said the Big Lady.

"That's a good idea," I said, lounging back in my chair with a smile: Go ahead, ask.

The woman looked me up and down, a little prickle of sweat on her upper lip. But she was cool about it, and when she left, shuffling briskly toward the swinging kitchen door she left a presence, an empty hole where she had been.

"I made Deena mad," I said.

Bea laughed, a real laugh, kind, but with humor. "Zachary, that isn't Deena." This was a new kind of smile for Bea, knowing, well-informed on some practical matters about which I was totally ignorant. "That's Ruth," Bea was saying, "and do you know what her hobby is?"

I could think of about a dozen bright things to say, but I was tired of looking at the reflection of the room in the polished hubcap, a smear of colors, humans wiggling along the edge.

"She listens to police calls on her shortwave radio," said Bea.

"I'll pick you up at six," I said, standing up, trying to make it all right by changing my tone, considerate, giving her a little chicken-peck kiss on the side of her neck.

"I think you better learn to operate your answering machine, Zachary," she said, pulling her blouse down hard, so BEA trembled at the point of her breast.

I thought about Bea all the way home, all the way into the kitchen, where I sat at the answering machine and listened to a line-up voices, one at a time, far-off associates of my mom's, most of them saying they didn't know what to say.

And sometimes Bea's voice was there. Bea, who didn't like to leave messages, was there like an ancient recording of a human voice, someone almost lost to memory. She didn't like to say anything straight out. She would say she was afraid of an onrushing avalanche by suggesting that we might not want to get our clothes dirty.

"It's three in the morning, Zachary," her recorded voice whispered. "I'm thinking about you."

I didn't believe Bea and I would ever be close in the way we used to be, but the sound of her voice on the answering machine changed the way I thought about my friends. I had been thinking that Bea couldn't possibly know how I felt. After all, I had been thinking, she had never even met my father.

I went into my room and booted up the computer. I sent Perry a message.

TWENTY

Perry's voice was on the answering machine early the next morning. I phoned him and got Perry's dad, a man who always sounded like he was a desert island and hadn't heard a human voice in weeks.

"Zachary, jeez, it's great to hear your voice," he said, crunching breakfast toast. "God," he interrupted himself, shifting to a more serious tone, like a sports announcer handed a grave news bulletin. "Perry told me." His dad expressed his condolences, a smart man who sometimes sounded dumb because of his enthusiasm for things, and then the telephone made a fumbling whisper and Perry was there.

I had the picture in my mind, Wheaties and muffin crumbs, a nearly empty carton of nonfat milk. I saw Perry in my mind, taller than me, tanned from exposure to the northern sun. Perry said very little, mostly uh-huh as I told him what I knew, doctors, IVs, cops. We were more comfortable snapping E-mail back and forth, voice communication clumsy and complicated, having to express everything out loud.

"This is awful," said Perry at last, and I felt bad about making him so solemn. Perry doesn't say *How awful* or *That sounds bad*. With Perry you get *This is true* or *This is bad news*.

I was happy to change the subject, just to hear Perry express some of his old interest in things. I said it sounded great, all of his plans, and we agreed that when this all got resolved maybe I could fly up for a visit, maybe look at the fish ladder, watch salmon swim upriver over a set of locks from salt water to fresh, all that Northwestern activity that sounded like life on another planet.

I was so happy to hear his voice, I went into my room and sent him an E-mail right away, letting him know how good it was to hear from him "voice-to-ear." But what I really wanted to tell him was to forget about kayaking and bear-tagging and take up an interest in sea otters or mule deer, some animal we have in California.

The water that runs out of a hose is sometimes hot as soup, even the brass nozzle gets hot. You can hardly touch it.

I let this first water run out of the hose for a while before I let it trickle onto the tendrils of my beans. Some of my beans were adult, nearly, having muscled all the way up the stake and then, with nowhere to go, spiraling down again. Only a few whiteflies danced around the pods as I splashed water over the plants.

What I saw next did not make sense.

The tomato plant, Mom's prize, was shivering. It wiggled, shuddering inward toward its stake. The leaves were nodding. Green tongues sprouted from the green rope of the stem.

I took my time, marching to the faucet, turning off the water, approaching the tomato plant cautiously. At times like this I find myself keeping up a running dialogue, like a cop chattering into his radio, except it's all in my head.

Okay, what is it, I queried myself. Some kind of disaster.

The plant was alive with fat green worms, each larva the size of my thumb, but longer, and when I stepped on one by accident it was green pulp inside, half-digested leaf. The sound of the feeding host of green caterpillars, *Hyles lineata,* was like rain heard far away. The fruit was untouched, green blushing orange, days from being fully ripe.

The dozens of swollen green larva of the white-lined sphinx moth were finishing the last foliage as I watched.

Not such a disaster. Nature at work. I wrapped my fingers around the tomatoes, and the fruit was warm, holding in the sunlight. I tugged at the fruit but the stem would not release, the vine wanting to stay the way it was. At last I pinched the tomatoes from the stems and hustled the armload into the kitchen.

The phone rang. I knew it was my mom. Mental telepathy was real, after all. A message had reached her: Big Green Worms Threaten East Bay. But I feel a tug of anxiety when the phone trills. Two inner messages hit me at once: answer it; let it ring.

Mom has an especially heart-stopping ring on her phone, an electronic police whistle. After four rings the answering machine kicks in. Two more rings to go. I could wait.

I picked up the phone without wanting to, my hand with a life of its own. I must have said hello because a voice was talking. He was glad he caught me at home. He was just heading out the door but he wanted to keep me posted.

What is it, I must have asked, because Detective Unruh's voice turned reassuring, sorry he had worried me. "It's not bad news," he said. But the way he said it made me want to sit down.

I heard the detective continue, his words massaging into me, a man proud of his voice without maybe being aware of it, aware that it was one of his strengths.

I interrupted. "You caught him."

Fit Pit was a gym you could see into from the street. I had tried not to pay attention to it before, a frenzied showroom stuck among storefronts on Solano Avenue, bodies running in place, pedaling, pumping iron. But as I stood in the doorway I could feel the activity pulling me in, people in a deliberate frenzy, tight smiles of effort on their faces. Others had no expression, sweaty stoics, rowing nowhere. I had expected thumping, urgent music, but there was only the iron chime of weights and the whir and beep of the machines.

A voice was calling to me, an inquisitive tone, nice but bossy, a woman's voice. I ignored it.

Bea was in a distant corner, slugging a great red punching bag with a pair of red Everlast boxing gloves. The bag was a little caved in from having been punched a lot in the past. Bea was punishing the big sack, her punches resounding among the whirring, clicking exercise machines. Bea didn't mess around with footwork, hooking her left fist hard into the red leather where it was worn black.

"I'm sorry," I said.

Whap. Her right hand caved in what was left of the bag's defense. And someone stepped around me to hold the bag steady, a woman with broad shoulders and eyebrows drawn on high above where her eyebrows would naturally be. She hugged the bag from behind, crouching into it.

"It's okay," said Bea. "He's my guest."

"He has to sign the waiver," said the woman.

I had insisted, telling Detective Unruh that I wanted to drive across the bridge, that I wanted to see the face, look into the eyes, but the detective used his voice on me, his calming,

Amazing-Grace voice, saying there was no need, everything was taken care of, he was just keeping me informed. I still insisted, and he said he was telling me to stay right where I was. Like an army officer in a movie: *This is an order.*

Bea gave the bag a rapid combination of punches, blows of such impact that the sound shook the insides of my body. She turned to me, panting, and wrestled her hand out of the glove. Sweat gave her face a strange gleam. "Sixteen-ounce glove," she said. "Try it on."

"The waiver form is over by the desk," the woman said. She was deeply tanned and her dark hair was gathered into a tousled bunch at the top of her head, one of those ageless people so well conditioned the tendons in her neck stood out.

"I won't be using any of the equipment," I said. I know all about waivers, promises that you won't sue if you drop dead. The interior of the glove was warm from Bea's fist.

"Let him go ahead," said the woman with the tough neck. She wore a black leotard top and shiny, tight stockings, shimmering and metallic looking. "Go ahead," she said, smiling. "I'll go get the waiver form, bring it over. A lot of people think they're in good shape until they give the big bag a workout."

"I don't feel like it right now," I said.

"It won't hurt," said the woman in the leotard, smiling so I could see her gums. She had smooth arms, hairless. Depilatories, I thought. She was engaged in life's endless war against hair.

Bea took my arm, sensing something about my mood. "Maybe just a rowing machine today, Sherry."

"This is your friend," said Sherry incredulously. "This guy who won't take a poke at the bag is Bea's friend." She gave me an I-don't-believe-it wave and sauntered off, giving me the full treatment, bending over to pick up a towel.

"What happened?" Bea was saying.

"You were gone by the time I came to give you a ride," I said. Ruth had even been friendly in a matter-of-fact way. "You missed her by about three ticks," Ruth had said. Bea must have done some explaining for me, told her about my dad.

"What happened?" asked Bea.

It should have been easier to say.

The gym was noisy, bodies grunting, the weight machines clanking.

Bea put her face up to mine. "They arrested the guy who did it," she said. Not asking, confirming.

I poked the big red leather bag, expecting it to move.

It didn't.

TWENTY-ONE

"The arraignment is Monday morning," said Detective Unruh.

It was Saturday afternoon, the day after my call from the detective. He was walking across the parking lot with a crumpled paper cup in his hand and looked back wistfully at the hospital entrance, unable to find a trash can.

I knew *arraignment,* pretty sure I understood what it meant.

A radio sputtered at his hip, under his dark blue jacket, cop-chatter turned down so low it was nearly inaudible. He unlocked a car I had not seen before, an avocado green Chevy. He slipped the mashed cup into a plastic bag labeled PITCH IN hanging from the dash. A notepad thrust itself from the dash on a metal platform, white, lined paper. A pair of empty brackets, one above the other, slightly ruined the appearance of a car where everything was useful and in its place. In the back seat was a Thomas Brothers map of the City and County of San Francisco, folded and tucked into a corner where, as he drove, the detective would never be able to reach it.

"The accused has a chance to post bond, hear the charge against him," said the detective, answering the question I had not asked. "He gets a court-appointed attorney if he needs one. Often somebody from the public defenders' office. Usually if the accused can post bail he can go free pending trial."

I glanced at the two empty brackets again and thought: where they keep the shotgun. "You mean they let him go free on bail?"

"No, a serious charge like this is an exception," said the detective. "He'll stay where he is."

Two cars were nose together in the parking lot, two men in shirts and ties hooking a jumper cable from battery to battery. Detective Unruh and I found ourselves drawn to the sight, like two people falling silent to watch an ad on TV.

"I want to go to the arraignment," I said, aware how dry and semi-embarrassed my voice sounded.

"No question about it, you have a right," he said, making a little speech out of his response. "The public is allowed to attend. But there's something I have to let you know."

Sparks snapped from under the hood, one of the men, the gray-haired one, shaking his head and swearing to himself. The younger man needed the help, and I could see his gratitude and irritation, how it troubled him that he had left his headlights on all day.

Detective Unruh turned away from the two men, as though

he couldn't stand to watch such amateur mechanics. "I think you might consider trying to be a little more detached about the legal process."

"The process will work, won't it?" I gave the word *process* a little twist: it's your word, not mine.

"There'll be a preliminary hearing, too," said the detective. "Usually it's just a few days after the arraignment, but in our case, we'll postpone it until your dad is well enough. At a preliminary the court hears the witnesses—in our case the only witness. The judge reviews the case the district attorney has against the accused, and decides if there's reason to hold a trial. In the meantime, our man is over in the new jail beside the Bay Bridge approach on Highway 101."

The younger man was in the car, turning the ignition, and the older one stood with his weight on one leg, hands on his hips while the ignition chattered, nothing happening. The two men were nearly the same age, I realized; the gray-haired man just looked older because he was heavier.

"In this case there might be some extra time involved," the detective was saying, turning back to watch just as the engine caught, revving, a loud sound from such a small car, a Neon or Tercel. The gray-haired man applauded, sarcastically or sincerely, it was hard to tell. "There might be a further delay, a week, ten days. We want your father to attend the preliminary."

The two men were out of the car, smiling, disconnecting the

pink cables. The thought of my father attending a court hearing confused me.

"We'll hold the preliminary hearing at the hospital," Detective Unruh said. "The fact is, we're going to need your dad's testimony. We've shown him pictures, mug shots, and he signals with his blink that he thinks this is the guy who shot him, but he isn't sure."

I let myself imagine it as a sequence of events, a mental video, hitting *pause* at the key events. My dad driving, stopping at a red light. Handing over his wallet, knowing money was only money. How loud had it been, the little pop, the gunshot.

"What's his name?" I asked.

The detective leaned back to give me a better look.

"The guy you have in jail," I said.

"He's in custody."

"His name," I insisted.

Little things about Hoover High bothered me, and when Perry left for the Great Northwest just before our junior year, I felt the pleasure I used to take in matters like locker combinations and accumulated tardies in the PE teacher's roll book begin to vanish. The problems I had with other students began to wear me down. Kids would fight in line at the cafeteria, throwing food at each other, the same kids, the swollen ears and fat lips still not healed from the last free-for-all.

Sometimes I got into fights, too, and I hated it even when I shoved back, face to face with someone way dumber than Earl. When I had the trouble with Mrs. Hean it was the final slap. I was excited about world history, eager to read up on trench warfare and the development of modern weapons. A machine gunner during the Battle of Verdun had a life expectancy of thirty seconds. You would find yourself on active duty in the war at last, squeeze off a few rounds, make sure the ammo belt was feeding properly, and then some Mauser from the trench three hundred yards away would lay a crease down the middle of your helmet. I elected to write my term paper on the history of the machine gun, from the Gattling on down to the Uzi, but focusing on World War One. I got the paper back with *You didn't write this* in jagged red letters in the margin, the grade a large, empty zero.

"I don't know what book you copied it from," said Mrs. Hean when I confronted her after class. "But it isn't your work."

I could have had Mom call for a parent conference. I should have had my counselor, Mr. Mendez, point out that my test scores showed me in the upper ninetieth percentile when it came to language skills, despite my so-so grades. I could have stood there in front of Mrs. Hean, a woman with a large, tan-wrinkled face and white hair, and tried to persuade her that she was confusing me with the students who downloaded their reports from some Web site at Yale or the Pentagon, but who would get away with it because they tended to come to class on time.

Instead, I felt insulted into silence, full of the sense that I was trapped in a school where loud and dangerous slugging matches were punished with half-day suspensions and good work was misidentified as the efforts of a cheat.

I stood there with the detective, watching the two cars drive off, one with a newly charged battery. I wondered what my life would be like if I could go back in time.

TWENTY-TWO

The evening before the arraignment my mom sliced the tomatoes. She put the slices on the white china plate that had belonged to her grandmother.

Fine cracks covered this yellowish old plate, the sort of china so fine it's translucent if you hold it up to the light. This was the first time my mother had eaten anything at home in several days, and it was good to have her there, the house shrinking to human size. It was a time like so many others, before my father was hurt. The rest of the neighborhood evaporated, and life was simple: plates, tablecloth, the two of us.

Mom sliced the tomatoes and then sat gazing into them, not digging in with a fork. She poked at the yellow tomato seeds with a tine, looking like someone who had heard about tomatoes but never actually seen one. I had not told her about the larva attack. I had pulled the tomato plants out of the tubs and thrust them into the compost heap under a tarp in a far corner of the garden.

I had kept a tomato for myself but chose to eat it like an apple, biting and sucking. It was delicious. A trickle of juice and seeds squirted out of the corners of my mouth, and ordinarily my mother would have said, "Napkin, Zachary," or "Eat it in the kitchen," not crabby but in charge.

Now she looked at me dabbing a seed off my chin and smiled, like she was happy at the sight in a weary way. It made me uneasy, this blessed-are-the-slobs attitude, and I wanted to goad her into complaining. I took a horse bite out of the tomato and sucked loudly. And she gave me a smile, a little tired, but real.

"I read him some Sherlock Holmes today," she said. She was wearing her aunt's cross, the cross that had survived the London blitz, and it looked delicate and old-fashioned glittering in the hollow of her neck.

I used a paper towel on my face. "Did he like that?"

"We used to read to each other, when we were first married."

Stories about the early days of their marriage tended to trouble me in an undefined way, how happy they had been in the student housing, former army barracks, badly heated. The two of them were new to each other, unencumbered by a child. But it didn't bother me now. She was just trying out a familiar subject, trying to maintain the quiet mood.

"I was going to cook some of my green beans tonight, but I

don't have quite enough," I said. I had made dinner, Shake 'n Bake chicken and Minute Rice. I wasn't proud of the cooking, but it was edible. The thighs and drumsticks turned out pretty good, all crispy.

"Sofia reads him the newspaper," Mom said. "The *Chronicle*. Sits there with it up in front of her face. She reads him the sports page. She reads the baseball standings. She does it badly, 'Mets one, Padres nothing,' on and on, not using any verbs." I could hear Mom's old impatience with Sofia lingering, coloring the higher-road detachment Mom was trying to keep.

"Maybe Dad likes listening to her—she could read the want ads and he wouldn't mind."

I had begun avoiding these visits to my father. Even when I wasn't working for Chief, I had reasons to stay home, weeds to pull, the front lawn to mow and then the back lawn, scattering nitrogen nutriment like handfuls of pink sand. You had to water thoroughly, so the chemical wouldn't scald the green grass.

After dinner Mom decided to go on one of her cleaning binges. The way she cleans house makes it more of an Olympic event than a chore, and I joined in. I vacuumed the living room, using the thin plastic nozzle to chase down the all-but-imaginary dust mice under the sofa, while Mom shook out the Persian area rugs and sorted through magazines, one pile for re-cycling, the other to keep in a banker's box in her home office.

I like vacuuming. When you suck up a paper clip there is

that long, musical journey up the metal tube, a rattling tour of the cloth portion, into the lungs of the Electrolux. I didn't do anything to spoil the matter-of-fact pleasure we were having, life the way it used to be, and even when she went through the closet for donations to Goodwill I helped her, knowing I could break the spell if I wanted to. I could argue that I wanted to keep the old Dodgers one-size-fits-all cap, or the foldable raincoat, used once long ago.

She huddled in the living room that night, talking into her portable phone, making notes. She wore one of her shiny bathrobes, dark blue silk, and she had washed her hair and wrapped her head up in a kind of turban, an old pink towel, frayed along the edges, that did not match her expensive robe.

I asked if could I get her anything, some warm milk with something in it, and she looked at me without saying anything, holding the little portable phone.

"You can't stay up all night," I said.

"They aren't putting their best person on the case," she said. "The district attorney's office. I've been trying to reach everybody and God but no one answers their pagers on Sunday night. An assistant DA named something like Dingleberry is in charge of the case. I did find out that the person they arrested is an Oakland resident, twenty years old, and that he has a record. Lives with his parents. They searched the house and did not find the gun, probably some cheap throwaway pistol anyway. A ballistics test won't be much help because the bullets are deformed and fragmented. You know who told me all that? The *Tribune*. It turns out when you need to know something you have to call a newspaper. Even the television stations aren't much help on Sunday. You know all those all-news radio stations. Try to call one up and talk to a reporter."

"We have to get some sleep."

She didn't even slow to take a breath. "At least one felony arrest, attempted robbery with grievous bodily harm, charges dropped. Insufficient evidence. They don't even take a criminal to trial unless they have an absolutely perfect case."

She stopped to consider what she was saying. My mom had always signed petitions and donated money on behalf of causes that were liberal, easing immigration laws, urging a more strict police review board. "You would think an assemblyman or state senator would have a staff on the weekends, someone you could call to put some pressure on the DA, but think again."

She was quiet for a while, and then she said, "One of these days we have to paint the ceiling."

TWENTY-THREE

The day I was arrested the sunlight was heavy on College Avenue. We were suffering one of those late summer, early fall days that settle in over the Bay Area and dry out every living thing. You get a spark walking across the living room, touching a doorknob. It was one week before school started, my junior year, right after Perry moved north.

Brush fires flickered on television, the Bay filling with smoke from a blaze near Point Reyes. It was a day that changed my life, but I can't remember where I was going, or why. I was wandering north, pausing every time I reached a shadow, past the upholstery shop, ANTIQUE ENGLISH AND AMERICAN, and the tropical fish store, poster-painted fish in circus colors on the plate glass. Three or four guys with a stunningly beautiful girl lounged all over the place, blocking the sidewalk, making a show of owning the thoroughfare.

I had gotten into fights and collected a few trips to the vice principal's office, but I still had a hopeful attitude toward school at that point. The truth was that I was wearying of summer and looking forward to a routine, relishing the idea of work.

I could have crossed the street. I bumped into them, shouldering through. One of them said something; I didn't even hear what it was. I spun on him and gave him my best stare. It's important to get it right, that mix of contempt and arrogance. And boredom, too. You want to look a little bored so if you have to back down you can act like it's just too much trouble.

The tallest of them gave me a little, preliminary shove. I took a step toward him, closing in, crowding him, getting way too close inside his personal space. Like I was getting intimate so I could whisper a secret.

He hit me with an elbow, the point of the bone right there on the lower lip. A sudden taste of warm saltwater blossomed in my mouth.

I spat in his face. The three of them were on me, holding on to me while the other hit me, and they beat me up, my face, my ribs, knocked the air out of me, stunned me, almost knocked me down. But then they got tired on that hot day, hard work, staying mad and getting all sweaty. When they slowed down, I picked one of them up and dumped him through the window of the tropical fish store.

Partway. The window spidered into pieces, but only one arm and part of his head punctured the shatterproof glass. When I tried to push him the rest of the way he kicked free, and we all sprawled.

It was the sure-handed humor of the police that really shook me. I was used to the vice principal's iron expressions, security guards breaking up fights, shouting. The police were almost amused, sure of themselves and calm, and that made it all the worse to be locked into a police unit. It was a cage car, with a grill between the backseat and the driver, the backseat made out of hard plastic, not cushioned at all, so if I was bleeding or puking I wouldn't leave any permanent stains.

My own trouble with the law was on my mind as my mom and I went to the arraignment of Steven Ray McNorr in room 211 of the San Francisco Superior Court.

To enter the courthouse we had to pass through metal detectors, like at an airport, except that the guards standing around are armed and look more like officers of the law. One of the tall uniformed men asked me to step over to one side for a moment while he passed a magnetic wand over me and up and down between my legs.

We had both put on our best clothes, like when we went to hear my mother's friend play Bach in an Episcopal church, and I imagined that the brass buttons on my navy blue jacket might have made an alarm go off.

"There you go," said the man with the wand, and I had that

feeling of being free to pass that I get from displaying tickets to a concert after worrying, for a moment, that I had left them at home.

Detective Unruh was in the hall, holding the door for a woman in a dark suit making her way on a pair of crutches. He turned, and when he saw us he smiled.

"My partner," he said, referring to the woman who had just vanished through the heavy swinging door. "She has to testify in a case involving a family who all started stabbing each other last Thanksgiving. Carving knife into the aunt, fork into the uncle." He pronounced aunt *ahnt;* in my family we say the word so it sounds like the name of the little insect. "She should be at home watching soaps. Instead she has to go sit outside a courtroom waiting for her name to be called while her codeine wears off."

I let the detective catch the look in my eye. "Of course you're here," he said. "I would do the same thing. Watch the law at work and let the law see you watching."

"I thought you warned me not to come," I said.

"If I ever warn you, you'll know it," he said.

Something passed between the detective and my mother, some adult understanding that both of them shared. Her manner toward him was muted, either by fatigue or by this mutual comprehension, when she said, "I've heard mixed reports on the assistant DA, Mr. Dingle—"

"Mr. Dingman. He's a good man to have on your side. We

can hope that Steven Ray McNorr will not see the light of day for a long, long time."

I took a seat in the back row, but my mother marched right up to the front, and I joined her there, comfortable seats, padded arms. The room was smaller than I had expected, and there were fewer people. A man in a sheriff's uniform wandered around like the room was his, a gun at his hip. The judge leaned over his bench like a man at work in an office, looking over to one side to consult with a woman holding a pile of folders, joking, words I could not hear, shaking his head in disbelief the way people do, *Can you believe that?* He wore a black robe.

I expected the courtroom to be very unlike courtrooms on television. I had expected real life to be more vivid, much more impressive. Instead it was like the courtrooms of movies, except that when something took place it happened quietly, off-the-record voices, paperwork, pauses while a computer hunted up a name, a date. I watched the judge, eager to learn from his expression what was going to happen. The judge was gray haired, and he wore half-lens glasses.

When a prisoner arrived I had no idea that he was a man about to be charged with a crime, just another person in the room, casually dressed in a pair of orange overalls. Only when he stood with his back to us and waited for the judge to stop talking did I see SF JAIL across his back, his hands cuffed.

But it was another name, not one I recognized. The words were spoken carefully by the clerk, first, middle, and last names. The man was charged with the crime of—but I was already not listening closely, people stopping by to murmur greetings to my mother and me.

Each time a prisoner was allowed into the room I felt wonderment—is it him? It was more than wonder—it was fear. I was afraid that when I saw the man I would not be able to control myself. But I could sense Detective Unruh's lack of interest, a matter-of-fact boredom that radiated from him like body heat. No one needed to tell me that this was some other human being in trouble, another criminal, another crime.

We sat there most of the morning. The flags on either side of the judge, California's Bear Flag and the Stars and Stripes, were both wrapped tightly around their poles, never stirring.

At twenty-five minutes past eleven the door opened again and another man was in the room, a uniformed guard on each side. He had dark eyes and dark hair, a square head, a square body. He sidled into the room like someone making his way through a crowd. There was no crowd. He was shackled, hand and foot.

No one had to tell me. Detective Unruh leaned forward behind me and whispered, his breath on my ear, "Here's our man."

TWENTY-FOUR

Steven Ray McNorr looked down and then rolled his head up so he faced the ceiling. He waggled his head from side to side, like someone with a crick in his neck, a boxer getting loose. He studied the floor again. It was taffy brown and pitted, years of heels bruising and cratering the surface. I thought, His eyes and mine, looking at the same worn linoleum.

A man in a sand-yellow tweed jacket stood next to him. The tweed was fine knit, a blue dress shirt showing at the cuffs. McNorr's breath was even, his shoulders rising and falling, under tension but getting used to it after the first few heartbeats. The words "assault with intent to commit murder" were spoken in a disembodied way by someone official.

"My client is ready to enter a plea at this time," said the man in the sandy jacket.

Plea. What a noble, old-fashioned word. You picture someone on his knees, beseeching, someone aristocratic, heroic, stripped of hope.

"How do you plead?" someone was asking.

McNorr looked straight ahead, not at the judge. His eyes might have been closed, and he might have been smiling or even weeping. But I knew—he had no expression. I could tell by the way he stood there, a man it would be hard to pick up or knock down.

One or two big strides and I could reach out and touch him.

He didn't even have to take a deep breath or clear his throat. He said, "Not guilty."

Detective Unruh's fingers dug into my shoulders. He leaned close to my ear. "Take it easy, Zachary."

There was nothing wrong with me. But when McNorr was shuffling toward the side door and the judge sat writing, lost in paperwork, I could feel it: my fingers almost cut by the edge of the chair I had been gripping, my body needing air. I had been holding my breath.

"Hang in there, Steve," croaked an older man's voice, and the prisoner looked up from the doorway and smiled. Smiled and shook his head.

I expected the judge or someone in a uniform to order silence in the court, but no one did. Two square, gray people, a man and a woman stood at the rear of the courtroom, the woman holding a small black book, one of those zipper Bibles you can seal against the rain when you're done reading. The man looked like his son, but gray, his strength melted to fat. The mother turned away before I could study her, a woman in a hurry to escape.

Sometimes as a child I would lie awake listening to my mother talking on the phone. When she was quiet, I would try to imagine what the other person was saying, hoping to time the imaginary conversation so it would end just as my mother couldn't restrain herself any more and bubbled over with, "That's what I'm telling you," or "See what I mean?"

I tried out another mental game at the hospital. I tried pretending that the patients were all right; it was the staff that needed help. Patients humored these warped, psycho people, pretending to be feeble so the nurses could get the therapy they needed, connecting IVs, plumping pillows.

"What an exciting day!" said the woman in white medical blouse, white pants, and white shoes. Her clothes were whiter than the uniforms of any of the nurses, who tended to wear gray blues and soft-soled, off-white shoes. This woman was as white as an aspirin, red lipstick, a chipped tooth. PERLA BEACH, said her badge. PHYSICAL THERAPY.

We were in the corridor carrying magazines, *Scientific American, Car and Driver,* glossy, colored periodicals we thought my dad would enjoy. "We just got back from the arraignment," my mother said, meaning she was in no mood for excitement.

"We've made so much progress," said Perla Beach. "There is some real cause for celebration, Mrs. Madison."

"Is there," my mother asked, flat, no inflection. You would never guess that Mom gave classes in the power of enthusiasm, sure to increase sales by thirty percent.

I left them, hurrying into my father's room.

He shifted his eyes in my direction, his face wrinkling into a mask of happiness.

Having rushed panting into the room, I found myself trapped by medical apparatus, tubes, cables, bumping a bag of what looked like black blood hanging beside my dad's bed. I found one of my mother's books on a side table. A bookmark, a clean, white cafeteria napkin, was folded over only a few pages into the novel.

"I don't think it would do me any good, hearing about a hound of hell from the middle of the moors," I said. "I mean, if I was sick."

Sick. What a frail, fake word to describe his condition. The breathing machine made its sound, air pumping in, pumping out, measured. The blue tube led to his throat, his trachea, and he needed a shave.

My jokey patter failed me. I took the book into my hands, one of those hardbacks embossed with fake gold to make it look more expensive. Where was Mom? I thought. Out there dueling with the therapist when she should be in here.

145

I opened the book. *Chapter II,* I read silently. *The Curse of the Baskervilles.*

That night I took a drive.

Sometimes nothing else helps, not music, not a long walk, not even the various antacids Dr. Wiegand recommends for Mom.

I picked up Bea at Deena's Diner, and she sat beside me as I drove, rubbing hand lotion into her skin, squirting it out of a tube. "If I don't I'll get iguana skin," she said.

I felt that Bea was hoping for a return to our personal Good Old Days, when we had spent the twilight together, gliding Frisbees until it was too dark and then holding each other, Bea's heart beating so fast it was like some living creature trapped inside her body.

I was grateful to have her as a friend, but I couldn't let myself experience any more emotion than I already was. "That might be interesting," I was saying. "Reptile Woman. Miss Gila Hands. Put you in one of those magazines, along with the world's biggest breasts."

My Honda was in good shape inside and out, the dark carpeting vacuumed with the wheezy Chevron One Stop Carwash vacuum cleaner, the armrests and the dash all wiped and polished. I had been driving the car for a couple of days after I got it back from the police when it seemed I could feel strange fingerprints on the steering wheel, unknown smudges on the floor mats. I purged the vehicle of this presence, wiped it down and cleaned it out.

I was down-shifting toward Taco Bell on Jackson Street in Oakland, when I saw Earl kicking a trash can into the street. I had not seen Earl since the night of the tear gas, and I couldn't help feeling a throb of friendship toward him. Good old Earl, the Lovable Barbarian.

I was about to roll down the window and say some kind of empty nothing, the sort of thing guys say to each other, *How's it going* or *What's happening,* phrases that sound like questions but are not. Two or three companions cheered Earl on, clapping, yelling.

He jumped on the trash can, log-rolling it, slipping off. He kicked the green metal so hard the top flew off and the bin rolled over and over, all the way across the broad street. The top was a peaked contraption with a swinging door on each side. People like putting their taco wrappers into a little swinging door, never seeing the trash again. The top of the bin sat upright, looking particularly truncated and useless in the middle of the street.

Earl was at the curb, punishing the bin with his feet. He began driving it back toward the opposite curb, Taco Bell wrappers and drink containers and unnamable junk tumbling and flowing as the bin made its progress.

One moment I was slowing down, running over some of this

coughed-up litter without wanting to. Then I was out of the car, seizing Earl, dragging him to the Taco Bell and slamming him against the wall. Bea's cry was lost in the night air.

The building shook, the posters taped to the windows shivering, jumbo flautas, half-price Pepsi, the glass trembling as I slammed Earl hard again and again. He was trying to say something, and that infuriated me all the more, his mouth parting and getting ready and saying something I could not make out.

His friends were grappling with me, weak claws, feeble blows. One of them knew me, some guy from high school calling out, "Leave him alone, Zachary—what's the matter with you?"

The look in Earl's eyes stopped me. Fear, of course, once the surprise was jolted out of them. And then something else. Something sickening. His eyes slipped out of focus. They didn't see me anymore.

I was hurting him.

T WENTY-FIVE

When the police took me to jail that hot day just before my junior year, I believed I was not going to see ordinary life for a long time. I was locked into a police car, both cops ignoring me, except once. We had to stop suddenly for a cardboard box rolling across Broadway. The police unit braked hard, and the driver looked back and said, "You okay?"

The police station in Oakland is like a post office, fluorescent lights, folders, desks covered with paper, nothing happening. You notice mostly what isn't there, no background music, no potted plants, the tack heads on the bulletin board red and white plastic lined up along one side, most of the bulletin board empty except for the faces of missing people.

The only other person they had arrested was the one I had spat on and thrown through the window. He wouldn't meet my eyes. He wouldn't look directly at the cop asking him to spell his name.

The fingerprint room was a surprisingly small chamber, signs

warning not to smoke. There were moments of surprising courtesy, a moistened paper towel to wipe the ink off my fingers,
being told there would be a restroom when we were on our way
to the holding cells "if we could just hold our water." That was
the phrase the cop-clerk used, but it didn't strike me as quaint or
comical. Everyone in that room down through the decades had
been aware of his bladder, a sac that can only hold so much.

The personnel acted polite in a leathery, impersonal way,
calling me Mr. Madison, maybe the first time I had ever been addressed that way. Before I could be showered or deloused or
raped a beefy woman was holding open the door, calling my
name. At the end of a hall my mother was standing with her
arms crossed, wearing too much makeup. I walked along beside
her, sure there was some kind of mistake. We were in her car before I could ask, and then I couldn't talk when I first tried.

"They dropped the charges," she said, sounding like a gang-
ster's mom, used to this.

She didn't start the car. We sat there staring ahead at a blank
wall, green cinder block.

"The owner of the tropical fish store," she said, "called up to
tell what he saw, you taking on half the East Bay. He laughed
about it. Can you imagine a business owner having a sense of
humor about a broken window? He said if you're going to get
into another fight, he wants to be in the front row."

I kept my mouth shut. I'd like to meet this man, whoever he was, thinking this was funny.

"What I want to know is why couldn't you wait?" she said. "Why couldn't you wait until you're eighteen and out of school before you decide to tear big chunks out of people. Because then you won't be my problem, Zachary. You'll be on your own."

I had to shut up and listen to this. It was music compared with what could have been happening that moment. Still, it hurt.

"It was the property damage that made them arrest you. You could stand and bash each other in the face all day and all night and it wouldn't matter. You break a window and they send in the Eighty-Second Airborne."

"I could have really hurt him," I said.

She was quiet for a moment. "I called the owner and said we would pay for the window. He told me he was glad you showed up, said the kids were a nuisance, blocking the sidewalk, keeping away customers."

I was in that mood I get into sometimes: I will never say another word again. I folded my arms, a family gesture, closed up and ready for the rest of my life.

She said, "You hungry?"

That was when my working life started, carrying bags of cement for a place that sold gravel and sand, paying back my mother for the window by putting in two or three hours after school. And then I worked for a nursery, stacking wooden pallets against a wall, chasing the raccoons away from the storage shed in the evenings, their brilliant eyes looking out from among the fuchsias. By the time I quit school I was ready to work full-time, hungry for it, wanting to put in long hours and forget.

After our drive down Jackson Street to the neighborhood of Taco Bell, Bea made us some instant onion soup, stirring it and pouring it into big stars-and-stripes mugs, dishwasher and microwave safe. Her mother was in San Jose with free tickets to a horse show featuring the Budweiser team from television and a team of mustangs descended from the wild horses of Nevada. My mom was spending the evening staying beyond visiting hours at the hospital. It was good to be in a house that was quiet but not empty.

"What do you think Earl is going to do with his life?" said Bea.

"What will any of us do?" I asked. I had meant to just hit the conversational ball back across the net.

"Do you think he'll get serious in another couple of years or stay the way he is?"

I couldn't think about Earl without picturing him almost losing consciousness, almost breaking the Taco Bell wall with his head. She must have read my thoughts. "Earl wasn't hurt," said Bea.

"He was," I said. "But Earl doesn't let a little brain hemorrhage slow him down."

We had all parted as friends, pals who were glad to get away from each other, picking up the trash in the street, laughing shakily, hey, we ought to have fun like this more often.

"And he was making a terrible mess," she said, "all over the road."

To me a "road" is out in the country, two-lane highways through hills and fields. Jackson was a street. Something must have shown in my eyes because Bea brightened, coming over to put her arm around my neck, holding my head to her slim hip. On a few other nights like this I had helped Bea undress, all the way down to her little boy's body, except for the bird's nest of fluff between her legs, and her petite breasts, pixie breasts, and I could hardly breathe I was so happy.

Tonight I was just glad to sit there in the kitchen with her, one of those times when the neighborhood is quiet and the one room you are in is like a space station, solitary but peaceful, all the experiments finished for the day.

"I almost forgot!" she said, scrambling to the back door, down the back steps.

The kitchen door threw a carpet of light, illuminating a pink garden hose and a snail in full sail. Beyond was all darkness, Bea out there somewhere, talking in her raspy whisper, scolding tenderly.

She bore something into the light, carrying it like an infant. "You hold him!" she said.

"Do I have to?"

"You're afraid!" she laughed.

I took into my arms the largest rabbit I had ever seen, big eared, black and white, and kicking, scratching my belly through my shirt. But then calming as Bea made kissing noises at it. I put it down, glad to have it off my hands.

The mammoth rabbit snuffled its mobile nose around the kitchen, taking no notice of our pant legs and shoes the way a dog would, browsing along the table legs and the wire from the toaster.

"I saved Carl's life," said Bea.

My mother had bought a yellow parakeet once, called him Pecker. When, as a boy, I asked why we couldn't have a dog, she would respond with stories of animals named Snout and Fuzz and Squats who ended up getting run over, in each case, "right in the middle of Ensenada Street." She kept the parakeet in the kitchen, until he escaped out the back door when she was cleaning his cage for the first time.

"Carl was drowning?" I asked. "Trapped in a fire?"

"I bought Carl from the Harveys."

Mr. Harvey was always having trouble with the zoning policies, the laws against livestock inside city limits. He had sued the city supervisors, claming his right to raise and eat whatever he wanted. When a group of South Sea Islanders were arrested for killing, roasting, and eating a horse one Sunday in July, Mr. Harvey was on television talking about religious freedom, even though he had nothing personally to do with the celebration in question.

She answered my question before I could ask. "Mom goes to the same acupuncturist as Mrs. Harvey."

Bea could always surprise me.

"The Harveys are very nice," said Bea.

I felt embarrassed, narrow-minded, ready to laugh at people I didn't know.

"Look, he likes you," said Bea.

I was swept just then with the warmest gratitude for Bea, thankful to be with her, gazing into the red eyes of the rabbit she held up for me to caress.

"Why?" I asked, not wanting to break the spell, "did you name him Carl?"

TWENTY-SIX

Chief drove in the slow lane, the truck sluggish with a jumbo load, quick-setting mortar in ninety-pound sacks, three top-of-the-line spa shells, three sauna installation kits, imported from Finland. We were rolling south, through the Santa Cruz Mountains, past Los Gatos toward Santa Cruz on Highway 17. The four-lane road was not big enough for the traffic it carried, even on this Tuesday morning, about ten-fifty-five, according to Chief's Timex.

When we took the Scott's Valley turnoff, Chief told me to watch for a road off to the left. "It shows up in two point eight miles," he said. "I watch the odometer, you watch for the secret passageway."

Redwoods closed in, brushing the side and top of the truck, a gentle scraping sound. "If we miss it we're lost forever," I said.

"You think it's funny," said Chief, like it was really *very* funny, but also true.

We caught the road without any trouble, a huge break in the

trees. The highway from then on was small, a winding route that followed a creek bed, rising and falling. Chief fought with the wheel, keeping the truck on our side of the road, slowing to let the occasional car pass us in the other direction. Once a lumber truck loomed and Chief had to stand on the brake. The lumber truck driver held a hand out the window of his cab, sorry to cause so much trouble, and Chief waved back.

Chief levered the truck into reverse, the gears grinding, and back up to a wide place nearly half a mile behind us. Even then the lumber truck had trouble, air brakes gasping, hairy redwood trees so close we could smell them, green life and cinnamon.

"You don't ever want to invest in a new truck," I said. "You want to drive this until it's ready for the Smithsonian."

"She's just getting broken in," said Chief.

The verge of the road was rutted where trucks had strayed off the pavement, and the asphalt was tracked with dried mud and starting to crumble, potholes spreading, burger wrappers in the blackberry vines along the road.

"Inevitable signs of progress," Chief said.

A creek lazed through boulders, the drought that made every summer dry cooking this water down to pools and dried scab, old algae, insects nipping the surface, a species I couldn't make out from a distance, mosquitoes or gnats. I could imagine my father's brisk insistence: a gnat is nothing like a mosquito, trying to be good humored about correcting me.

I spied a black-winged damselfly over a puddle, a tiny, darting needle stitching in and out of shadow. I imagined myself capturing it with the fine-mesh net and bringing the winged insect to his attention, crying, *Look*.

I could close my eyes and hear his voice. Whether he kept the insect for his collection or not, he would smile and say, "That's a real specimen, Zachary."

I drove all the way back from the construction site.

Chief lost a lens out of his glasses. After we both looked around among the boxes of ceramic tile and paper sacks of patching plaster, we gave up the search. I kept praying we wouldn't meet any oncoming trucks on the narrow road, and we didn't. By the time we reached stop-and-go traffic at the turn-off for the Oakland airport, I was getting used to the old truck, enjoying the feel, up above the rest of the traffic.

When I got to the hospital late that afternoon the first thing Perla Beach said to me was, "We have good news."

I was a little tired from pumping the clutch all the way from the Santa Cruz Mountains, and I was unable to pick up her unspoken message, the brighter-than-ever way she talked. All I could think was: were her clothes new, or did she use bleach every time she did the wash?

My father blinked.

"Zachary," he said.

The respirator made its constant, airy noise, oxygen in and out.

"Detective Unruh said his partner had a relapse," said my father in a high, squeaky whisper. I put my hand out to a bright metal pole and a plastic bag of clear fluid swayed back and forth.

My father swallowed, a struggle, and said, "Her pins got infected." A pause. "But she'll be okay."

T<small>WENTY-</small>S<small>EVEN</small>

"Sofia says the insurance company was very sympathetic. The agent was really helpful. She's getting a new car," I said, thinking: I'm chattering again. "It's just like the other one, only a couple years older. And a different color. Sahara sunrise or Sante Fe something."

"Great," he would whisper, waiting for the machine to breathe out. If you asked him a question while the air was flowing in he had to wait, like someone speaking on a radio from another planet.

"You don't mind? About the color?"

He made no response, his eyes reading my face, intent on what I was not saying.

I kept talking. "I haven't ridden in it yet, so I don't know what kind of shape the upholstery is in. If there's a problem, I'll rub mink oil all over it, give it a good treatment."

That was the typical kind of thing I talked about, padding out the safe subjects of cars and gardening. My drive back from the

Santa Cruz mountains was good for half an hour of one-way talk, how hard it was to change lanes when you were driving a truck, but how much you could see, higher than the rest of the traffic. Sometimes, though, Dad laughed, a silent parting of his lips, his eyes closing, opening, no sound, when I imitated Chief's walk, like a bantam rooster, or Perla Beach's expression, cross-eyed with enthusiasm.

Mom read the Sherlock Holmes novel, stopping to comment, "You're lucky Dr. Watson isn't your surgeon," or, "I think Holmes was guilty of criminal negligence—his client nearly got torn to pieces." Mom had the lean look of a tennis player over the hill but refusing to retire, experiencing life as an endurance contest, popping Excedrin when she thought no one was looking.

Sofia could talk of Daniel, what new video he had picked out to watch the night before, what bad dreams had awakened him. Sofia didn't look so sexy these days, puffy and pale, looking like someone who has just gotten up from a restless nap, no matter the time of day.

My grandparents passed through one warm day, flying up from Florida. My grandmother is a woman so calm and pretty, in a delicate way, it is easy to forget that she is deaf and unable to hear a word. She talked about subjects that required no conversation, her trip to Russia at the height of the Cold War, the weather where she lived, how hard it was to keep a boat in the water in Florida for any length of time, the barnacles ate everything alive.

My grandfather is a man so handsome he looks like a model, someone constantly showing off what today's seniors are wearing, golf shirts and pleated twill pants. Only when I took the time to talk to him did I notice how unsteady and unceasing his smile was. They left after only a short visit, their eyes not sure where to look, but sounding upbeat, saying medicine can do wonders.

Dr. Monrovia grew a beard. At first he had a seedy, derelict appearance that made him look hungry and even dangerous, until you realized it was only Dr. Monrovia, back at last after being marooned on a desert island. Gradually he began to look distinguished. One portion of his beard was white and the other dark, the white patch crooked, as though he had been eating powdered sugar and needed a napkin.

Dad was in a new room in a different wing of the hospital. The new ward was quieter, fewer nurses, fewer patients. Wheelchairs waited beside beds, and nurses helped people on crutches out onto a terrace, junipers in big clay urns.

The doctor said Dad was still in pain, headaches he never complained about to me, "an expression of the damage done." When I asked, the surgeon explained that there was no lingering injury to his head. "It's just that he has no sensation in his body, and there is nowhere else for the pain to go." Medication blitzed the pain, Valium and Demerol, but they left Dad's eyes drifting, wandering from TV to ceiling to nothing, focused on a zero point.

That first remark he had made to me was something he had prepared, practicing with Perla Beach's help. Detective Unruh's partner's surgical pins had become slightly infected, the bones not healing as quickly as they should. She was expected to recover, and it might have been a sign of my father's state of mind that he found another person's medical problems most worthy of comment.

Some evenings Bea and I went down to Lake Merritt, but the police were enforcing a curfew. New lights illuminated the oaks and redwood trees around the lake, and the water seemed unusually low, dark stones exposed by the receding tide. Bea's hair was growing back, and sometimes she looked completely different to me, someone I did not know.

Some evenings we set up the badminton net in the backyard. Bea and I swatted the birdie back and forth as the twilight held off, not a plastic birdie, but a traditional, feathered specimen, one Mom had bought for a title company picnic at Tilden Park. Sometimes a neighbor's cat crept in to follow the shuttlecock with his eyes, lunging when the feathered thing bounced close, swatting at it, looking up at us with keen puzzlement each time he rediscovered what it was.

I got good at spiking the birdie over the net, striking it with the racket's sweet spot, and Bea fired it right back, as good as Perry used to be. During these games there were no thoughts, no messages, nothing but the game, no one keeping score, Bea and I lunging and laughing, trying to keep the fluttering white shape in the air. Afterward I would put my arms around Bea while moths scribbled the dark.

One afternoon as I arrived home from work, an envelope I had been dreading was there in the mailbox.

A snail had made it all the way up the mailbox post, and stuck. I pried the shell off and could see the gastropod tucked way high up inside his shell. I set the creature on the curb where it probably would survive, tugged open the mailbox, and reached in.

I ignored the multicolored junk mail, platinum credit cards wanting my mom's business, charities she supported telling her it was that time again. There was only one envelope that mattered. It was from Laney College, the word TESTING rubber-stamped under the printed address.

I told myself I wasn't worried. I went into the bathroom, peed, washed my hands. I stalled further, tugging off my Ben Davis work shirt and putting on a clean gray T-shirt, before I picked up the envelope again.

I went into my room and sat on the bed before I opened it. When the envelope was torn carefully, one end gingerly ripped off, I slipped the letter all the way out and left it facedown on my lap.

I think I even prayed, a few muttered words, before I turned the letter over and flattened it against my lap. Even then I kept my eyes out of focus. I wished that I were one of those people who need reading glasses. I could fuss with a pair of spectacles for a few more seconds before the truth was in my eyes.

He parted his lips, his eyes full of questions.

"The Graduate Equivalency Exam," I told him again, aware of how little this might matter to him now.

He licked his lips. This was beginning to be a tick, something he did without thinking.

I held the letter up so he could read it and waited while his eyes followed the sentences along. He had always been a fast reader, but now his eyes returned to the letterhead, searching the three short paragraphs. When we brought him magazines someone else did the reading, holding up the pictures for him to see. Reading was probably something he had not done since the shooting.

He sees the words, I thought, but they don't make any sense to him. He's farsighted. Or else his brain can't translate the symbols anymore, the injury giving him aphasia, like a stroke victim. He frowned slightly, parsing out the sentences, ashamed to admit his disability.

165

TWENTY-EIGHT

"Which one do you think?" Sofia asked.

"When was the last time he wore this?" I asked, fingering the lapel of a blue striped seersucker, one of those suits you take one look at and think: mistake.

"Never," she said. "He bought it for a conference in Greece one summer, but then there was a strike at the Athens airport and the meeting was canceled."

My dad's suits were displayed on the bed, five of them. They were sinister, headless ensembles waiting to turn into men. My dad was not usually comfortable in traditional men's clothes, preferring to wear khaki field clothes, denims, all-cottons that absorbed sweat and were easy to wash. But he gave lectures and met with supervising committees, explaining why another grant for research on the life cycle of the medfly was a must.

The house my dad shared with Sofia was one of those buildings with too many windows, a view of cypress trees out one side of the bedroom, the Bay out another side, glass everywhere.

166

Daniel was watching television in a distant room, a sound of explosions and screeching tires as the housekeeper's voice reached us, asking him, didn't he want to watch Goofy.

"What did he say he wanted to wear—gray or off-gray?" I asked. "Or maybe this nice granite gray."

"He just said he wanted argyle socks."

The legendary argyle socks that had brought him luck years ago must have been long ago worn through to so much string. I doubt Sofia understood the full implication of his request as she found a pair of Byford knee-high wool stockings in his top drawer.

"I bet he didn't insist that he had to wear a suit," I said.

"I said I'd pick out something handsome," said Sofia, looking a little lost among jockey shorts and V-neck T-shirts.

I pulled open the closet door, a storage room big enough to walk into. His field boots were lined up in the half dark, along with other shoes, burgundy loafers, shiny black dress oxfords. I chose a pair of crisp brown pants, what a commanding general would wear going to war. I found a cotton dress shirt, fresh from the cleaner, still in its plastic wrapping.

"Which shoes?" Sofia asked.

I had already selected a pair of nearly new loafers. I imagined one of the nurses having to tie shoelaces, my dad having to endure being dressed by someone he hardly knew.

———

Was I trespassing? I told myself I wasn't, but why did I wait there in the hall? I barely nudged the door to his office, letting it swing open.

Sofia had turned off the distant television and was giving instructions, vanilla pudding only after Daniel ate the green bean casserole for lunch. The beans were from my garden, and Sofia had created a novel and tasty meal that Daniel would chew but would not swallow.

His study, my mom would have called this room, enjoying the fact that her husband was a scholar. But Dad would have called it his fort, finishing his tuna salad and saying "back to the trenches." He would spend hours peering through a binocular microscope, examining the jugular lobe of a wasp's wing.

But I had never spent more than a minute or two in this newer working place, the one Sofia must have helped him set up. It looked like the office of my childhood, aside from the updated computer and printer. Books and journals were haphazard if you glanced at them, but they were arranged to be within easy reach, the Audubon guides to everything from trees to mammals just beyond the Merck Manual and his brace of dictionaries, English, German, Latin. And there was, as always, the slight smell of mothballs, the camphor that protected some of the hundred-year-old specimens of monarch butterflies.

I found Sofia holding up scarves, letting them fall one by one to the floor, scarlet, uranium yellow, brilliant silks, gaudy pat-terns.

"You didn't deal with his mail," I said.

Sofia gave me one of her pretty looks, eyelashes and incom-prehension, but I could tell that she wanted to be alone.

"There's a gigantic pile of envelopes you haven't even opened," I said.

"I paid all the bills," she said, "and I opened anything that looked like a get-well card."

"But there's all his journals, and articles people have sent him, and catalogs, and announcements—" Weeks worth. It was a crisis, all the work that had piled up.

"It doesn't really matter, does it?" she asked. She let a long gauzy silk drape over her arms and held it up so the light fell through it, studying the way the room looked strained through silk.

Jesus, I thought. *Doesn't matter.*

"He can't remember," Sofia said.

She glanced to see the effect the words had on me.

"He can't remember the shooting," she said. "He thought he could help the police, but he can't."

A painting was slightly crooked on the wall, an acrylic, a scarlet mountain. There was art in every room of the house. Sofia's parents made money manufacturing patio doors.

"It's normal to have retroactive amnesia regarding a very bad trauma," she was saying. "Many people can't remember the events just before a very grievous injury." She let the silk scarf fall to the floor.

I slowly shifted the objects on the dresser from one place to another, jewelry box a little closer to the mirror, bust of Pasteur toward the edge of the dresser, beside the pearl necklace. Dad had won the bust in high school for his ant map, a chart of the paths worker ants took from the insect colony to a cube of moistened sugar. The bronze had a slot in the base if you turned it over. You could use it as a piggy bank.

I found myself able to ask, "Does the detective know?"

"He suspected as much."

"They should postpone the hearing until Dad feels better," I said.

"It's been almost a month," she said, "since the arrest."

"They can use hypnosis," I heard myself offer. "Put him in a trance and record what he says."

Sofia gave me a look of kindness before she shook her head.

"They can give him more time," I continued. "Let him get back to being more like his old self."

Sofia tucked the underwear and socks back into the drawer and closed it very gently. She nudged the bronze Pasteur back against the mirror.

TWENTY-NINE

There was another, more subtle reason for walking away from high school, although I didn't like to admit it. Mrs. Hean and the crude, ignorant fellow students weren't altogether to blame.

Somewhere inside I knew that I could never be like my dad—urbane, knowledgeable, someone who flew all over the world to tell people what he thought. I was playing my dad's game by staying in school. It was a sport he would always be better at than I was.

Bea brought one of her books along to the hearing at the hospital, a dog-eared insight-into-the-mind paperback, but she never opened it, sitting with the novel in her lap the way Steven Ray McNorr's mother sat with her Bible. Bea must have expected that the preliminary hearing would take all day, with many breaks and many sidebars, the judge conferring with attorneys, the sort of long delays Court TV fills with expert commentary.

I wished I had brought something to read, too, a way to keep my mind off this slow, unreal passage of time. Bea and I sat together but we didn't talk much, both of us silenced by the procedure around us, a bailiff with a holstered pistol making sure the folding chairs were lined up straight in the brightly lit hospital conference room.

A court clerk said, "Raise your right hand."

The witness had thin white hair, combed straight back, and his hand twitched on the crook of a cane. The hand he held up to swear to tell the truth was gnarled and had a slight tremor, a vibration that never ceased throughout his testimony.

"Shall I sit here?" the witness asked.

It was not such a ridiculous question. The judge was not behind a bench, only a table with chrome legs. The judge was dressed in a dark suit. The court recorder sat looking up vaguely, fingers ready at his machine. The witness's chair looked like an afterthought, a piece of furniture left there by mistake, one of the few wooden chairs in the room.

"Yes, that's fine, Mr. Van Kastern," said Mr. Dingman.

My father's eyes were steady, watching the witness. The truth, my father must have been thinking—now we will hear what really happened.

The witness looked at the chair, put a hand out to the chair's arm, and let himself down into it in stages, getting his body settled, arranging his pants front free of wrinkles, finding a place for his cane. He put a hand to his bolo tie and gazed up at the assistant district attorney with a desire to please so keen it was nearly a smile.

Mr. Dingman, the assistant DA, had tight brown curls all over his head, like a scrub pad. He led the witness through the questions with the sympathetic voice a man would use on a child.

The witness's name was Wiebrand Van Kastern. "People call me Weebs."

He was a retired jeweler who still helped around the shop on Nineteenth Avenue. He had been born in Amsterdam, in the Netherlands. He had trained in Geneva as a young man, learning the repair and maintenance of time pieces. "Real watches," he said. "No batteries." He was a naturalized U.S. citizen, but he had an accent, American with the spice of other places. He had lived in San Francisco for thirty years.

"You're the owner of Golden Gate Jewelers, aren't you, Mr. Van Kastern?" asked Mr. Dingman.

"Yes, I'm the owner," said Mr. Van Kastern, a man who didn't like to brag. But there was a trace of impatience, too.

It was the first time I had ever seen my father in a wheelchair. The chair had gray rubber tires, plump, with a knobby tread, like a child's bicycle. The shirt and pants I had picked out looked good. His shoes gleamed with the unnecessary touch of Kiwi neutral polish I had given them. His hands were on his knees, unmoving, a yellow canister of oxygen in a wheeled rack like a luggage carrier beside him.

Sofia's eye makeup was too dark. Mom wore dark glasses and a black scarf. She was burning up the vacation days she had saved for years and was considering a leave of absence. I could tell when she was looking at me by the twin wrinkles, one in each cheek, all she could manage of a smile.

The witness was telling us what he had seen that Saturday, just past noon. Mr. Van Kastern had been changing the display, setting out Seikos and putting the Pulsars into a drawer, getting ready for a sale.

Mr. Van Kastern had seen what happened outside in the street. A young man had approached a Mercedes at the stoplight. He saw the young man bend over the driver's side of the car.

"Do you see that man in this room today?"

The witness pointed to the defendant. McNorr wore a jail jumpsuit, but his hands were not cuffed.

"Let the record show that the witness has identified the defendant," said Mr. Dingman.

McNorr was leaning on his elbows, one hand on a sheet of paper, like someone taking an exam, working a problem in his head.

"What happened then?" Mr. Dingman asked.

"Then?" asked Mr. Van Kastern.

The defendant picked at the paper, loosening a staple.

"I heard a shot," said the witness before the DA could repeat his question. He said this assertively, his voice rising, as though recounting the event made him experience his surprise again, his rush out onto the sidewalk. "The Mercedes rolled through the red light and collided into some cars parked along the street."

"And what else did you see?"

"Running."

"Did you see someone running from the scene?"

"I saw *him*," said the witness, emphasizing the last word, his eyes steady behind his glasses. McNorr pinched the staple, worked it loose, the paper tearing slightly.

McNorr's attorney wore the same sandy tweed as before, a man with pink cheeks and smart, quick movements, smiling, putting his hands in his pockets, not wandering all over the room like lawyers on TV, but leaning over the table. His voice was pleasant, his manner polite.

The witness had not seen a firearm in the hand of the defendant. The witness had not seen a gun go off. The witness had not seen blood, had not seen a wound.

"No," he answered each time. No, he had not seen the witness dispose of any weapon. He had not seen a wallet in the defendant's hand.

Mr. Van Kastern was able to answer *yes* to some questions. Yes, he had medical problems, and, yes, he was due for cataract surgery next month. The witness suffered from arthritis that affected his joints, and he had trouble moving quickly. "Have you been diagnosed with hearing problems?" asked the attorney.

Mr. Van Kastern turned to the judge. The judge told him to answer the question as honestly as he could.

"I don't hear as well as I used to," said Mr. Van Kastern after a long moment.

"Why did it take you so long to report what you saw to the police?" asked the attorney.

"I had to think," said Mr. Van Kastern. Then he looked over at Mr. Dingman, an expression of apology, as though another answer to this question had been rehearsed and forgotten.

"What was it you thought about?" queried the attorney.

"I had to think about what I saw," said Mr. Van Kastern, but there was defeat in his voice.

Bea put her hand on mine. I knew what Mr. Van Kastern meant. When a terrible event takes place sometimes the mind has to climb back down inside itself and study the episode.

When the judge said that it was time for a recess, I sat there, not moving, my eyes closed, listening to the steps shuffling out, the room emptying, the wheels of my father's chair squeaking on the floor.

———

I put my hand over my father's hand, before I remembered that he could not feel my touch.

"We're just heading back to our room," said the nurse sweetly, meaning: get out of the way.

Dad had trouble focusing. His face was blank with fatigue. He found me with his eyes as I knelt down beside him and told him everything would be all right.

THIRTY

Detective Unruh searched for the right package of sugar, as though each were unique. "Nothing," he said, answering Bea's question. He snapped the packet of sugar back and forth, then tore the one corner. He poured the contents into his coffee. "Nothing happens."

"They aren't going to let the killer go free," said Bea. She was unable to keep herself from saying what she really thought and for an instant was tight-lipped with chagrin. She believed my dad was as good as dead.

"Free," Detective Unruh echoed, relishing the word without joy. "He'll be out in a day or two. Home watching the soaps with Mom and Dad." He had that brisk attitude people show when they are wise to the world and you aren't.

"What should we order?" asked Bea, picking up a menu.

"The food here is pretty good," said the detective. "My favorite is tod pramuk, a calamari dish, great stuff. Here they fry it up tentacles and all; some people don't like that. I think it's tasty. It's got that special crunchiness." He gave the last words a special lift, like someone making up an ad.

"I like squid, too," said Bea. "But I'm not hungry."

"You're hungry for this," he said. "Deep fried squid for three?" When we didn't respond he said, "The pork satay is good here, too."

"The DA's just going to forget about the whole thing," said Bea.

The detective put on one of his Lecture Faces, about to say something he had planned ahead of time, probably on the drive over after the hearing broke up. "I wanted to take you two out to lunch so I could have a chance to talk to you seriously," said the detective. "Because I know how disappointed you are in what happened this morning."

"The witness was telling the truth," Bea said.

"I think he was," said the detective. "I have no doubt. But you see how weak he is going to be as a foundation for an entire case."

I could feel the weight of his attention, but I made no sound.

"That's why they have preliminary hearings," he continued, "to see what kind of disaster you might be facing if the case goes to court."

"Mr. Van Kastern saw the crime take place," Bea said.

"I know it. The DA knows it," said the detective. "Everybody knows McNorr was the shooter. But our case is like the house built upon the sand."

"You told me he wouldn't see the light of day for a long time," I said in a quiet voice.

"I said we could *hope*. I had a sense of this case from the beginning, what kind of problems we contemplated," said the detective after studying his empty sugar packet, a little color picture of a Hawaiian beach.

"Maybe you can go out and interview more witnesses," said Bea. "Maybe find some evidence."

"I feel it, too," he said. "I feel that kind of anger all the time. But I go on living. On the other hand, it's not my dad sitting there in a wheelchair."

I sat very still. Maybe, I thought, after a very long time, I might reach out one hand and pluck one of those C & H sugar packets out of the container.

"You don't look at me when I talk to you, Zachary," said the detective. "You know that?"

I kept quiet.

"You can look at my face once or twice. I used to be like you when I was your age. You don't believe that, do you? That I look at you and see myself?"

The waiter leaned in from the shadows, a soft voice asking us if we needed more time.

"More time," said the detective emphatically.

When the waiter vanished, Detective Unruh leaned in my direction. "I want you to talk to a counselor."

I unlocked the car.

I used to wonder what it would be like to be one of those men who never talk. It used to seem that little boys jabbered all the time and cried when they scraped a knee, while a certain type of man never complained.

"People go into prison," she was saying, "and come out and do it all over again."

I drove. The Bay Bridge traffic was skittish, a traffic jam broken up at last, everyone trying to reach the speed limit without getting killed. A large plastic garbage bag bounded along in the middle lane. One more bounce, and a semi loaded with scaffolding flattened it. I glanced in the rearview; it was gone, and I couldn't even see what was left of it.

"Mom was buying a new chicken-wire cage for Carl," she said. "He was too big for the other one."

I was glad to be driving, very carefully, like when I took my Department of Motor Vehicles test, a man with a clipboard in the passenger seat saying not *hello* but "Before we do anything, we have to do what?"

"Carl definitely needs a big cage," I said. I drove like someone in a training video, *Traffic Safety and You*. I signaled before

I changed lanes; I kept a safe following distance between my Honda and the other cars all the way across the Bay Bridge.

"I argued against keeping him in an enclosure at all, but we have some cats in the neighborhood. You know how they are," she said, as though following an inner command: whatever you do don't shut up. "It's not their fault. But we have to be practical."

"No cat is going to be able to handle Carl Jung," I said.

I swing the car over to the curb, a sprinkler playing water over her front lawn. It was late afternoon, country music twanging along inside the house. Detective Unruh wanted me to talk to a social worker, someone who specialized in victims and their families.

"You better come in," Bea said.

I must have shaken my head.

I could see the argument she was about to make. "Mom was going to make chili. Not the kind that is so hot you have hiccups for an hour. A sweet, New Mexico–type chili she got out of a magazine."

Before you do anything, the right answer was, what you do is buckle up. You could drive perfectly and if you didn't do it with your seat belt on, you would fail the test.

We both heard it—a masculine laugh from inside the house, one of Rhonda's men.

———

The bean plants were gone, nothing but brown twine and bare poles where green plants used to thrive. I used a pitchfork, working the garden. I got on my hands and knees and broke the ground with a tool like a steel claw, three prongs. When I surprised an earthworm, I was careful. It isn't true that slicing a worm in half makes two living worms.

Mom brought home some lemon chicken and bok choy with black mushrooms. We ate with wooden chopsticks, the kind that come stuck together. You snap them apart, and it never works quite right; they are always a little jagged and splintery where they had been joined.

She said, "Daniel drew a picture of a man with fire coming out of his head."

For a person who tells people how to organize an office, Mom spends a lot of time alone. Dad was the one who made friends easily, men and women wandering in and out of his life. He had hiking partners and bird-watching friends and pals who liked to shoot holes in a National Rifle Association slow fire pistol target.

Mom called her contact at the *Tribune*. McNorr was still in jail.

The next day Chief and I delivered a spa shell and a filter system to a condo in Albany and drove the old spa and rusted motor to a scrap dealer in West Oakland, a block away from the Nabisco plant, the smell of toasted wheat in the air.

When I got home that afternoon the phone was ringing. Normally I wouldn't have answered it.

It was Mom. She said, "They let him go."

THIRTY-ONE

I already knew the name McNorr was not listed in the Pacific Bell White Pages.

Day by day I had been getting ready for this, flipping through the phone book, calling information.

The phone in the kitchen kept ringing, the answering machine picking up after the third ring, but I could hear what people were saying, if there was anything they could do. I tore up the junk mail, taking a liberty, figuring Mom wouldn't mind. Then, with the Macy's bill in my hand, I had an excuse to step into her office.

Mom's home office tends to flow out into the dining room. She keeps multiple listing books and tax records tucked into boxes, but she prefers to spread out. A desk calendar featuring architecture of Julia Morgan perched beside an electric pencil sharpener. Mom likes a number three pencil, very sharp.

It was my way of making a deal with Fate: if I can't do it, I shouldn't.

I slipped off the dust cover and let it parachute to the carpet. The tough plastic cover kept the computer's shape perched on the floor, covering nothing. The old IBM took awhile to boot up, making the usual clicks and chuckles, getting ready. When I was on-line, connected to the main computer at the title company, I entered *owners/Oak,* just to see if the computer's internal watchdog was asleep.

When it said *Enter passcode* I knew the first part would be easy, my mother's Social Security number. I have a memory for data like phone numbers and scientific names, and I was quick, tapping out the nine digits. But then I needed a three-letter or three-digit code. Guesswork.

I tried my mother's maiden name, shortened to *Gan* or *Gnt,* and each time the computer was prompt in telling me *Please reenter.*

Maybe the McNorr family didn't own their house, I told myself. Maybe the computer was programmed to deny all access after the third attempt.

I could hear Dad's voice clearly in my imagination, my dad coming home early when I was home after school, first grade and already reading faster than all the others. I remembered how he sounded, singsong, telling us he was home, calling out Mom's name.

I tried again, two-fingering the nine numbers, and then, after the dot, not Flo. I entered Ren, short for Renny.

Often I could read her mood by what she put on when she came home. A bathrobe meant she was ready to relax, drink one of her cocktails, a whiskey sour, an old-fashioned, watching trash on television. If she put on denims and her Green Bay Packers T-shirt she was going to wax floors or paint walls. When she came home that night, she put on a dress, like someone getting ready to go to a party, something dark and flowing, a dress I did not recognize.

"Something your father talked me into buying," she said. "When we were first married and couldn't afford it."

"It looks nice," I said, careful to keep my tone steady, no feeling in my voice but casual courtesy. She needed a compliment, and that's what I would give her. But the luster had gone from her hair, and she looked frail, even her hands, chapped and thin.

"It was never in fashion," she said, "and it was never out of fashion. I almost never wore it."

"You rented a video?" I asked, noticing the cassette in her hand. Mom was patient with computers and could go toe-to-toe with an accountant, argue depreciation schedules and deferred payments until she got her way every time. But she was always jamming cassettes in backward and pushing the wrong button

187

on the remote, calling my name when the screen was all dancing fuzz.

I took the cassette from her hands.

I sat in my room, on the bed, telling myself I couldn't really hear it.

The sound of his voice pulled me into the living room.

"What we imagine might be taking place on a distant planet," my father said. "The sort of being we dream might be thriving in a distant galaxy is living right beneath our feet."

He knelt on one knee, smiling up into the camera. "Right here," he said. "On our Earth." Was it makeup? I wondered. Had he really looked so tanned, so strong? He was like an actor hired to impersonate my dad, someone too handsome, not at all the normal human being who paced up and down the living room, trying to memorize the lines he had written for himself.

"These accidents of nature have lasted five hundred million years nearly unchanged. These remarkable invertebrates are citizens of prehistory." This was no actor. This was Dad, the enthusiasm in his voice, his joy in sharing what he knew. "When we spy a common little black ant, the imposingly named *Monomorium minimum,* stealing sugar from the kitchen sink, we are looking down upon one of the triumphs of the animal world, an animal so old and so perfectly adapted to its life that it has not changed since the extinction of trilobites."

People wanted to watch cheetahs run down gazelles, the PBS executives said. Viewers loved wolves, and bears, and sharks. "Scarabs," one assistant producer had suggested in a fax from LA. "The dung beetles of ancient Egypt. People love mummies and pharaohs. Work up that angle—the mythic sacred creatures of the Nile."

Dad laughed off the failure of the PBS pilot of *Prehistoric Future*—or at least pretended to. The book it was based on was translated into six languages. You could see his faith on the screen, the way he scrambled up a cliff, the Steadicam following, so he could show the viewer a crevice in the sandstone where wasps were hibernating. "They are cold-blooded creatures, and even our mild winters make them slow down to a crawl," he said, his shadow falling over the stones.

"When they wake," he said, "they will not have to learn or experiment. They will not have to be told. They will know exactly what to do."

When it was over we sat for a while.

She got up, turned off the television, and looked around at the living room, appraisingly, like someone house-sitting for a neighbor and tired of it, ready to go home.

"I told Sofia I would stay with her tonight," she said. She made an expression of ironic fatigue. Mom used to call her *Sofa*, saying it was the perfect name for someone so good to lie on.

But I knew that Mom's kindness to Sofia had little to do with Mom's gradual acceptance of Dad's second wife. It was a way of helping Dad, a way of working against her own feelings to do something right, even though it meant she was searching the medicine cabinet for antacid, painkillers, settling for a packet of Alka Seltzer so old the tablets barely fizzed.

THIRTY-TWO

I told myself I was just going for a drive, no particular destination.

I found the street without any trouble—Olive Street, where it meets Foothill Boulevard and runs east toward the 580 freeway and the big quarry gash, a landmark you can see even at night in the Oakland Hills, soil and stone ripped to bedrock.

The houses in that neighborhood have metal grills over windows, double doors, filigrees of iron it would be hell to cut through. Dogs bark. Men on street corners watch passing cars.

But at last I reached a quieter part of town, not far from the freeway. I had trouble locating the addresses. Some of the houses had metal numbers attached beside the front door, or glittering on the mailbox, but some did not.

I felt conspicuous in the early evening, out of place. I coasted very slowly, nearly stalling. An out-of-date Ford rusted on the front lawn, on blocks, a white Galaxy. A pickup truck, hood up, occupied the driveway, the garage door open only

MICHAEL CADNUM

enough to allow a person to leave and enter. The interior of the garage was dark.

Geraniums flowered up under the picture window, and the curtains were open. The lawn was black in this poor light, a hedge on either side of the house, and a big shrub, something that was not thriving, snaking stems and broad shiny leaves.

No people. The front window—what Mom would have called a "picture window"—was empty, the wall across the room pool-bottom blue. A car approached, headlights in my rearview mirror. The approaching car's sound system thumped, bass notes all the way through my body. I jacked the Honda into gear and cautioned myself to keep under the speed limit, twenty-five, maybe thirty miles an hour.

I passed the house again and began to wonder if they had all gone out to celebrate, leaving the lights blazing, fooling the would-be burglar. Once again I drove around the block.

This time I let the Honda kiss the side of the curb, stopping, holding my breath. The curtains swayed and began to close in little jerks. The curtains stuck. A figure edged into the narrow space between the curtains, an arm reaching up to adjust one of the hooks that attached the drapery, the person standing on tip-toe, muttering with the effort. I knew how he felt, having to fuss with such a mundane annoyance on a night like this.

A light flooded the garage, the door open only enough for

me to see a shadow moving around on the concrete floor, a can of Budweiser glittering beside the pickup truck.

I drove, letting the car find its way.

Deena's Diner was crowded with cheerful, hungry people. The special was lettered on a white plastic squeak board, the kind Dr. Monrovia had used to illustrate my dad's injuries. Bea was handing out plates of Caesar salad, plates of vegetarian enchiladas, the two specials for tonight. She gave me a dazed, weary smile, and I could see how satisfied Bea was with her life. She loved this shuffling of orders, the hectic, blackjack dealer side to being a waitress. She liked all of it.

Maybe I had been hoping for some event to deflect my intentions, someone to say just the right thing, some random comment to stop me. But I wouldn't try to talk to her. I waggled my fingers and mouthed, *I can't stay.*

I stopped by a corner grocery on Piedmont Avenue and bought a carton of bean dip and a jumbo bag of Doritos. Just before I gave the cashier the money I hurried back and got a can of tuna off the shelf.

I ate standing up at home, over the kitchen sink, scooping up the bean dip and then eating the tuna out of the can with a fork.

I washed my hands, wiped my mouth and chin with a paper towel. I called Chief's number, and Harriet answered.

"Tell Chief I won't be in tomorrow," I said.

"Bernie is so upset," she said, a voice that sounded like a singing voice, a contralto, round voice, even though she was only chatting on a phone. She liked the sound of her voice and depended on it to keep her listener right where she wanted him. "We both are. We look around at the world we live in and just don't know."

Bernie.

I forgot to tell her how much I enjoyed her sandwiches. It wasn't quite true, but I wanted to say something polite. I hung up too soon.

The spade was in the shed with the dregs of the lawn nutrient, the nearly empty sack tangled up in the blade of the spade. I stuffed the large paper fertilizer bag back into the shed and then listened to the neighborhood, the televisions, the muted conversations, the background hush of far-away traffic.

The lime tree drops leaves all year round. Once a week or so it lets one fall, tinted with yellow. Mom called up a nursery and they told her this was how a citrus lets go of used-up leaves, little by little, not all at once like the birch or the ginkgo.

I dug into the ground with the spade, the steel chiming and grating against the tiny bits of gravel and concrete in the soil. I took care, not quite sure, digging with my fingers, wondering exactly where.

Deeper than I expected, I remarked to myself. Maybe not here at all.

I was thirsty, even a little queasy. Okay, it isn't here. Brilliant, another great moment in the History of the Mind. I felt giddy, an audience inside me, a theater with no applause, no laugh track, flat silence.

The plastic bag did not make the rustling sound I expected. One moment I was spading dirt. The next minute the steel met steel, a dark sound, too loud. I fell to my knees and worked with my fingers again, uncovering the weight.

THIRTY-THREE

I filled in the hole, pressed the dirt with my shoe, and put the spade back into the shed. I closed the shed door and slipped the latch over the loop where a padlock was supposed to fit if we had one.

Details were all that mattered. How I made my way across the lawn, careful not to step on any snails, how I wiped my shoes on a stepping stone, scraping off the dirt—each specific detail had an effect on what I was going to do.

I had seen his father at the window, reaching up to hook the drapes so they would close. I made up a story, what they were doing now. Watching videos, Steven in the garage, drinking too much beer to be much of a mechanic, but loving it, back at home. The initial flush of freedom was probably already fading, little things starting to bother, Mom's sulks, Dad's stupid choice of television reruns. Mom keeping her mouth shut, her son barely escaping the law again, Dad more philosophical, figuring cops make mistakes.

I could picture Steven Ray McNorr's hands, fumbling for a Phillips screwdriver, prying open another beer, his fingerprints dark smudges on the King of Beers.

I cradled the gun in both hands, the barrel pointed toward the floor, away from my body. As I entered the kitchen, Rhonda Newport was being processed by the answering machine. "I bet your family has a civil suit," she said. "Sue the shooter for gross bodily harm." Her voice paused, trailing upward, questioningly.

If I was home, she was saying without coming out and asking, pick up the phone. "Zachary, believe me I know." She didn't have to say what she knew. Rhonda knew her way around the buttes and gullies of life, even the ones she had made up herself. I let her talk a little more, enjoying the way she sounded, ice tinkling in one of her poodle highball glasses. She hung up.

The Vaseline was so thick the cross hatching of the walnut grip and SW trademark were obscured, the weapon ugly with petroleum jelly. I used sheets of paper towel, sitting in my bedroom, gently wiping the barrel, the trigger guard, afraid I would drop the thing or grab it the wrong way. I wiped my hands on the paper towels, using up what looked like half the roll.

No signs of rust. Still loaded, I prompted myself, as though working my way down a checklist. Scared at my own nerve, I gave the cylinder a turn. It clicked, clicked again, and stopped turning.

My nerves jittered at every murmur of the house—the fridge,

the floorboards breathing tiny, subsonic sounds. The walls had a silence so solid it was a sound itself, a background presence, the hush of a canyon.

I put the gun on the breadboard. I thrust the Safeway bag into the trash under the sink with the wads of paper towel. I washed my hands. I couldn't get the water to run very hot, but I used plenty of dish soap at the sink. Even then some of the lubricant remained. I let the sink half fill, running soapy water through my hands, until they were clean at last, not a trace of Vaseline.

A car breathed by in the street. The kitchen faucet dripped, once. The gun looked so dark and outlandish here in the kitchen I could hardly bear to put my hand on it. When I placed it carefully in the middle of my bed it pressed down on the mattress. I hurried into the bathroom and peed. I checked the mirror, my normal look, maybe a little flushed. There was no way you could tell.

I put on a Gortex jacket, a bulky blue garment with several pockets, a jacket fit for a trek through a blizzard. Mom had bought it last Christmas, just before our visit to Squaw Valley, where Mom liked to talk shop on the ski lifts, interest rates and boardroom gossip at seven thousand feet.

The gun settled into the pouch in front, and the pocket's tab fastened shut, the miracle of Velcro. The jacket felt too warm. I zipped it up, zipped it back down. Its bulk almost offset the pull of the gun, and I was all the way to the car before I thought: speed limit. Traffic cop. *Step out of the car, please.*

I opened the trunk and folded the jacket over the spare tire. The gun clunked against the tire iron even through the fabric of the jacket, and I folded the garment gently into the corner.

I don't believe in reincarnation, but sometimes it is a theory that explains everything. I must have practiced all of this before, rehearsed it well, in another life. I took 580, the freeway light traffic all the way. The car was running fine, and I had two-thirds of a tank of gas. Then I made a miscue and took the Fruitvale Avenue off ramp, having to drive all the way down to Foothill Boulevard again.

That feeling of being in no hurry was gone. Keeping the speed limit was an effort of will. The ordinary act of driving, stop signs, clutch, gearshift, was slow, way too slow, the car rolling along with something wrong with it, the tires out-of-round, the parking brake stuck.

My hands slipped on the steering wheel, the porch lights and bedroom windows I drove past lurid, mockingly normal. I could still turn back. It was a gift I had saved up, and now presented myself. Good news—I could go straight back home and take a shower.

How could I act like I had done this before—this exact series of actions, parking the car a few houses down, making sure my headlights were off, opening the trunk to tug on the bulky jacket. I even knew to press the gun against my body, determining its position in the pocket, loosening the Velcro but not reaching in, leaving the actual walnut-and-steel untouched a little while longer.

The only physical sensation I paid any attention to was thirst. I ached to dash up one of these gravel-and-juniper front lawns and drink from a garden hose. A dog barked, one of those yammery little dogs no one pays any attention to. A woman opened a front door across the street, arguing cheerfully with someone inside, shutting the door again after pouring out what remained of a pitcher of water.

The garage door was still open just enough for an angle of light to spill out on either side. The car was parked in the driveway, beyond the light.

The beer can was gone, a new moon of condensation where it had been. The truck's hood was down. The door on the driver's side was open, a new beer can standing right about where someone would plant his foot climbing out of the cab. I could tell by the beads of moisture the can was three-quarters full.

Even then I was giving events a chance. It might be someone else in the vehicle, the dad or a friend, or even the mom, enjoying her hobby, replacing the alternator in the family truck.

I could not take another step. A human being nearby made a grunt, effort or muffled violence, sex. My insides shrank, my hand reaching for the outline of the gun. The sounds came from the pickup.

Someone was inside the truck, the soles of his feet jerking and straightening as he worked under the dash. An oblong of light searched the interior. I slipped into the shadow beside the garage and put one hand on the sharp stucco edge of the building.

He half fell out of the pickup, knocking over the beer. He didn't notice the spreading pool of fizz, the yeasty fragrance. He peered at a glittering object the size of a cigarette butt in his fingers. He held the flashlight, examining a fuse from under the dash.

The light from the flashlight exaggerated his features, his eyebrows lurid black, stage makeup. But I knew that square build, that square head.

The Velcro did not release at first, clinging, a harsh, sandpaper rasp. I tugged a little harder, peeling the flap just as he looked down at his feet. The flashlight illuminated the dishwater mess of spilled beer.

THIRTY-FOUR

I stepped on the accelerator so hard the car shimmied in place, no forward momentum, tires squealing.

Red lights didn't stop me. Stop signs meant nothing. I was in fourth gear over eighty miles an hour on Foothill Boulevard before I was aware of any other traffic. A yellow Cadillac Seville with a row of holes in it where the chrome strip had come off swerved over to me, two grinning guys saying without words if I wanted a contest I was in the right place.

I cut across the four lanes of city street and into a neighborhood, switching back and forth for several blocks, and the three hundred horsepower Cadillac attempted to follow in a half-joking, half-menacing way, blundering behind me until I careened around the back of a strip mall, Dumpsters and bales of flattened cardboard.

I wasn't sure where I was, parked cars crammed along the

curb, broken glass on the pavement. A Doberman on a chain ran along with the car until his leash yanked him. I slowed way down, feathering the brake. Two police cars were in conference, back to front, the drivers nearly touching elbows.

I kept driving, past the Oakland/Alameda County Coliseum, a street sweeper gliding along in the distance, its headlight illuminating the empty parking spaces.

The Oakland Airport is at the end of a plain of dry grass and ditches, reeds and sleeping mallards. I ran the car off the road, over the shoulder, broken glass and trash crackling. I wrenched open the door, and ran up an embankment. The rumble of a jet receded into the sky as the night air hit me.

I took a step back, swept the gun behind me, and threw it. I didn't just toss it or skim it across the water. I sent it with all the strength in my body. I could see the light from the runway glinting, spinning.

I didn't hear the splash.

I got on the freeway heading north and rolled down the window. I was sweating, wet with it, breathing hard. I wrestled out of the heavy jacket and shucked it over the back where it made noises as I drove, collapsing its empty arms and body further down into the dark.

———

A restaurant commanded the freeway with its sign, TWENTY-FOUR HOURS A DAY, a place Chief and I had passed but never visited. I found the off ramp, parked at the edge of the lot, and found myself outside the coffee shop. Newspaper machines sold *USA Today,* the Sacramento *Bee*. The night air was unfamiliar, heat and farm smells, manure, and something else, irrigation, water among orchards.

PLEASE WAIT TO BE SEATED. Three people were ahead of me, shuffling along to a side table where they had a good view of Highway 80. Someone turned a chewing face in my direction. I was still cold. It was a mistake to come in here, all these eyes, and these weathered faces.

Half the coffee shop must be looking at me by now. I found an empty place at the counter. My wallet was jammed with crumpled money. The currency was stuck and would not respond to my spastic attempts to pull it out.

"Coffee, hon?" said the waitress.

I nodded, please.

She poured the Farmer Brother's brew fast, a method I admire, throwing the coffee into the mug all at once. But I rarely drink coffee, thinking of it as a drink for people so addicted the caffeine has little effect. She set a glass crammed with ice on the counter, and I drank until the ice made a noise when I sucked it.

"Are you okay?" asked the waitress. Concerned—interested, even. But there was a hint of criticism, too.

"Do you have Cobb salad?" I asked.

I could have gone to the men's room but I didn't want to see my face. I left before my order arrived, leaving money beside the knife and fork.

THIRTY-FIVE

They polish the floors of a hospital with a machine that glides. The operator clings to a handle like a power lawn mower, the newly buffed floor shining. He sets out little signs, WARNING, WET FLOOR, a swath of light where the machine has passed.

Maybe I expected someone to stop me, so early in the morning. Maybe I expected the institution to be closed, forgetting that it never shut down, open twenty-four hours a day. Visiting hours, I was thinking. *Come back later.* People would look at me and know there was something wrong.

But they ignored me, the woman with the clipboard, the bald man on the phone. I passed by like someone who wasn't there.

Maybe I took a wrong turn, distracted by a Pepsi machine, thirsty again, no coins in my pocket. I was lost in a room of weight machines. Over by the window was a big yellow spa, Olympic size, a brand I had never seen before.

———

"I took it easy on the garlic," she was saying. "Perla said it might cause gas."

The door was open but I knocked anyway. The sound turned Sofia into a statue, Woman with Spoon. She was holding a Tupperware bowl on her lap, and a long stainless steel spoon was dripping onto the floor. Dad had a napkin on his front, sitting in his wheelchair fully dressed, the same pants I had picked out for the hearing.

"Zachary, Florence is frantic," Sofia said at last. It was rare for Sofia to refer to my mother by name, not *your mother* or *she*.

I had interrupted something between husband and wife. I considered leaving. Maybe the weird sensation I was experiencing was hunger.

"She got home around midnight and you were nowhere," Sofia was saying.

I made a show of calm, finding a chair, the metal legs stuttering against the floor tile. I didn't sit down yet, my knees feeling stiff and unreliable. "Minestrone for breakfast?" I asked. My words came out hoarse, leathery.

"Call your mother," said Dad.

A drop of soup had stained the baby blue napkin tied around his neck. I located a chair in the corner under a pile of professional journals, some of the mail he was getting around to at last.

"Don't bother sitting down," he stage whispered. "Go call

Flo," he said, the respirator forcing him to pace his words. "And tell her you're all right."

Sofia looked away, blushing a little, maybe embarrassed to be suddenly a part of a family fight.

"You make it with ham hocks," I said. I knew how I sounded. I was buying time, making conversation. "Cook it two or three days. I had it once, remember? That time Dad and I came back from the Marin headlands cold and wet. We had captured a rare butterfly, the Muir hairstreak, in a grove of giant cypress. I thought your soup was the best stuff I had ever tasted."

She smiled at the compliment but didn't put much energy into it, her mind on other things. "I didn't bring the right spoon," she said. "This one keeps dribbling."

His pants needed to be ironed. The room had a stale, medicine smell, a smell like plastic, a TV fresh from the store.

"You're not," he said, waiting to get in rhythm with the breath machine, "going to sit there like that."

My dad had no right talking to me like this, especially in front of Sofia. In a minute or two, I told myself, I would get a paper towel and wipe the drops of minestrone off the floor.

Dad gets this expression on his face, a silent shout. This was my dad's usual style, Mr. Agreeable until he gets impatient. Sometimes you hope people will evolve, and they don't.

I left the room, and this time people saw me, lowering a clipboard to say something, looking up from the waxing machine. It didn't matter. I was leaving. Outside I hurried across the parking lot, like a man I read about once who had caught himself on fire and couldn't stop power-walking out of town as fast as he could, keeping a few steps ahead of the pain.

But I did stop, finally, and watched a sea gull pecking at a squashed wrapper on the sidewalk, spearing it, taking it away. If I make a video someday it will be about flies and vultures, how we shouldn't hate them. A man wiped his windshield with a towel, tilting his head to catch the angle of light off the glass. Cars started up, exhaust feathering into the cool morning.

Until I die I will remember: I stepped out of the shadow while Steven Ray McNorr unzipped his pants and peed, a long, steaming arc into the hedge beside the driveway.

He never saw me. He took his time, shook himself off and tucked himself back into his pants. It took a while, the zipper snagging. Then he slammed the truck door. He had trouble finding the right key, while I watched with the .38 in my hand.

And couldn't use it.

THIRTY-SIX

"They are going to be here in forty-eight minutes," Mom said. She was already dressed in something flowing and red, her thinking being that shades of scarlet were going to be her color from now on. She had begun using dye on her hair.

"They can see me the way I really am," I said. I was on my knees, pulling weeds. Wet soaked into my pants from the moist soil, and something about the smell of lawn was satisfying.

"Try, Zachary. Please."

With the arrival of the winter rains, the nutrients my mother had been scattering for months began to take effect, and everything that was a part of the lawn grew abundantly, including the weeds. Front lawn, back lawn, I was on my knees filling a cardboard box with crabgrass, devil's grass, dandelions, and cockleburs. Then I had to rake the clawed places in the lawn, and when I was done I saw all those unnamable weeds in the seams of the sidewalk and dug them out with the point of a screwdriver.

"I don't want him to see it like this," I said.

"You aren't even pulling weeds at this point, Zachary. You're scraping moss."

Bea had loaned me one of her books, three hundred pages on the theory of personality. I was beginning to feel that maybe I was a classic introvert in a world that would not shut up. I had promised Bea that she could meet my dad.

Dad was able to read, despite my earlier fears. I sent him E-mail almost every day, using a new computer Mom scrounged from her office. Dad was fitted with an attachment for his glasses, an infra-red point he used to direct a keyboard on a computer screen. He was beginning to write about the creature he had always loved. "Ten percent of the earth's biomass consists of the nation of ants," his first chapter began. I could tell this was going to be one of his best books. He could only work on it for an hour or two a day before he got too tired.

"Finish up, go in, and wash your hands," my mother was saying. "I mean, just a suggestion. And put on some pants that don't have what looks like green snot on the knees."

Now that my father was out of danger, Perry's messages tended to be about glaciers, wolves, and how the mother grizzly's milk is twenty-five percent fat. Over Easter he was coming to the Bay Area with his dad, arranging to sell their old house. We were planning a hike to see the tule elk herd at Point Reyes.

"I didn't want to wear heels," she said, trying to be patient with me, and wanting me to hear the effort in her voice and appreciate it. "But these flats are too Little-Bo-Peep. Don't you think?"

It was my dad's first visit since it happened. It was his first visit anywhere, aside from a few hours watching television at home with Daniel. He had shaken off two bouts of pneumonia during the last four months, and was on a new antibiotic. Sofia was trying out their new van with a hydraulic lift. I had bought a sheet of half-inch-thick all-weather plywood and put it down over the front steps as a ramp for his chair. Mom and I had spent the morning rearranging furniture and working wrinkles out of the carpet.

When I swept off the sidewalk, I saw that there was really nothing more for me to do. I wondered what it was going to be like to have him here. I wondered how painful it would be for him, the stairway, the back garden. Sometimes I woke at night and couldn't sleep thinking about him, straight through until dawn.

Why hadn't Mom planted some shrub that flowered this time of year? The begonias along the stepping-stones to the house looked pathetic, drunk with winter weather.

I washed my hands. It wasn't a simple matter, getting the dirt out of my nails, soaping and rinsing, and then thinking: maybe I should have showered. But by then there wasn't enough time. I put on navy blue pants and a blue chambray shirt. Then I took it off and put on a cream white shirt with blue checks, something Dad hadn't seen before. I kept glancing at the digital clock in the bathroom, the travel clock on the dresser, the heirloom pendulum timepiece tick-tocking on the bookshelf in the living room.

Five more minutes.

Sofia promised they would be on time, but how could they keep their word with traffic on the bridge the way it usually was?

"I think I should wear that Peruvian hand-crocheted Pima cotton thing," I could hear Mom saying. "And those sterling and tagua nut drop earrings."

"No, you look great already," I said.

"Or pearls," she was saying.

Of course they would be a little late. And Dad might want Sofia to take a detour so they could take a look at where he used to buy milk and beer when he lived on this side of the Bay. He might take her by the playground where I had thrown up from playing on the swings too long, five years old and no concept of motion sickness.

Mom had met with her lawyer, Billy Brookhurst, considering a civil suit against McNorr. The lawyer took her out to dinner, took her to the opera, but in the end he said the case wasn't strong enough. At first I drove by the McNorr residence once or twice a week, slowing down. The last time I passed the place there were red and yellow tricycles on the front lawn, and a plastic baseball bat.

"Make sure the coffee table is all the way at the end of the room," Mom was saying. "Are you sure the kitchen door is wide enough?"

"I measured it," I said. A week ago, and this morning, using both a ruler and a steel power tape. The doorways were all wide enough for his chair.

My mother has a talent for anxiety, the way some people have beautiful voices, or a sense of humor. She even gets me worrying, her nerves contagious, like yawns.

I put all my weight on the plywood ramp, balancing. The ramp was steady. I rehearsed it in my mind, how I would push him up the ramp into the house, talking all the while, so neither of us would be self-conscious. I would mention the bonsai tree I was thinking of buying, how the dwarf maple had lost its leaves, just like the full-sized trees all around.

He would ask for the scientific name of the maple, speaking in that practiced whisper, and I wouldn't know. He would ask, What kind of a botanist are you going to be if you can't master a few Latin names, sounding upbeat, but making his argument felt. He would tell me the garden looked good, even if it didn't, keeping a hold on my feelings.

They were late.

It wasn't sunny, it wasn't cloudy. A neighbor kid was yelling, not in pain, not in anger, just making noise. I walked out to the curb like a person going somewhere far away, just as soon as his ride came around the corner.